GOOSEBUMPS HorrorLand™
ALL-NEW! ALL-TERRIFYING!
Also Available on Audiobook from Scholastic Audiobooks

GOOSEBUMPS®
NOW WITH BONUS FEATURES!
LOOK IN THE BACK OF THE BOOK
FOR EXCLUSIVE AUTHOR INTERVIEWS AND MORE.

HELP! WE HAVE STRANGE POWERS!

R.L. STINE

SCHOLASTIC INC.
New York Toronto London Auckland
Sydney Mexico City New Delhi Hong Kong

ISBN 978-0-439-91878-7

Goosebumps book series created by Parachute Press, Inc.

Goosebumps HorrorLand #10: *Help! We Have Strange Powers!*
copyright © 2009 by Scholastic Inc.

12 11 10 9 8 7 6 5 4 3 2 1   11 12 13 14/0

Printed in the U.S.A.
First printing, April 2009

3 RIDES IN 1!

HELP! WE HAVE STRANGE POWERS!

Sometimes being a twin totally rocks, and sometimes it's the pits.

I hate all the jokes. People say, "You look so much alike. How can I tell you apart?"

That's supposed to be funny, see. Because I'm a girl and my twin is a boy. Ha-ha.

Our parents didn't help us out. I mean, naming us Jillian and Jackson. That's too cute for words, right? I've been thinking when I get older, I may change my name to *Adrianna*.

Or do you think that's too snobby sounding?

Well, I'm stuck with Jillian for now. But I don't let anyone call me Jilly or Jill. And I never wear the same color clothes as Jackson.

I guess I'm more sensitive about the twin thing than my brother. He's the relaxed one in the Gerard family. Everything is cool with him.

Mom says I *think* too much. It sounds like a compliment. But she doesn't mean it in a good way. She says if I were a superhero, I'd be Worry Woman.

Jackson and I are into superheroes. We're saving up our allowances to go to the big comic-book convention in San Diego next summer.

But that's a whole other story.

Jackson and I are twelve. We both are tall and thin. We have wavy brown hair and dark, serious eyes. I'm on the swim team at school, and I like to play tennis, and I take horseback riding lessons on Saturdays.

Jackson is into sports, too. Mainly, *Madden Football* on his PlayStation 3.

Dad says Jackson should get up off the couch and get more exercise. Jackson told him, "I'll get a lot more exercise if you buy me a Wii."

This argument goes on and on.

Anyway, one good thing about being a twin is you always have someone to go to the movies with. One rainy night after dinner, Dad dropped us off at the tenplex at the mall. We ran to the ticket window to make sure *Butt-Kicker II* wasn't sold out.

Butt-Kicker is our favorite superhero. He started out as a member of the Mighty Mutant Club. But he was kicked out for being *too tough*!

How cool is that?

Jackson and I bought big buckets of buttered popcorn. Then we made our way down the aisle of the crowded theater. We like to sit very close

4

to the screen. We don't like people to come between us and the movie.

We sat down on the end of the third row. I stared up at the screen. Basketball players were leaping about a mile off the floor. It was a commercial for sneakers that could make you "almost" fly.

"Great seats," Jackson said, digging into his popcorn. "I don't mind a stiff neck — do you?"

"Of course not," I said. I accidentally bumped his arm with my elbow. A little popcorn spilled onto the floor.

"Hey — watch it!" Jackson snapped. He twisted away from me. "This is my new sweater. You'll get butter on it."

"Jackson, it's a *black* sweater," I said. "The stains won't show."

Jackson didn't reply. He was staring past me to the aisle. And he had a horrified look on his face.

"Oh, noooo," he moaned. "I don't believe it. Oh, noooo."

And that's when all our trouble began . . . on the day Jackson and I got our strange, new powers.

I turned and saw Nina and Artie Lerner squeezing into our row.

It was my turn to let out a groan. Jackson and I can't *stand* those two kids.

I wanted to pretend I didn't see them. But Nina was already waving to us. And Artie had a dopey, toothy grin on his face.

They dropped into the seats next to Jackson. "Funny meeting you here," Artie said. He giggled. That was his idea of a joke.

"These seats are too close," Nina complained. "It's making my eyes hurt."

"What is this dumb film, anyway?" Artie asked, wrinkling his thick black eyebrows. "Is it like Batman or what?"

I took a deep breath. "Butt-Kicker could eat Batman for breakfast," I told him.

Let me explain about Nina and Artie. They are twins, too. And they just moved to our school in September. We're in some of the same classes.

And because they're twins and we're twins, Jackson and I were assigned to be like their school guides. You know. Show them the ropes.

So we became their first friends at school. We really didn't want to be their friends. We quickly discovered they were both totally gross and disgusting. We didn't like them at all. But people were always putting us together.

You know how there's one kid in class whose nose never stops running? Well, that is Artie Lerner. Artie and Nina both say they have sinus problems.

But Artie is the worst. He's constantly blowing his nose into these disgusting, wet, wadded-up tissues. And when he eats in the lunchroom, snot drips onto his sandwich. Really!

How gross is that?

Artie is always giggling at things that aren't funny. And he thinks he's cool because he wears baggy, low-riding jeans and long, heavy metal rock-group T-shirts. But no one is into that at our school. He looks like a little kid playing dress-up!

They both have curly brown hair that looks greasy. And they walk kind of hunched over with their shoulders slumped. They look tense and worried all the time.

The Lerners have high, whiny voices. Nina never stops complaining about her migraines and her sinuses and whatever.

She stands too close when she talks to you. I mean, right in your face. And she always pokes you with one finger as she talks. She's always touching you, and grabbing you, and poking you.

I guess you get the picture. The Lerner twins are no fun.

Nina squirmed in her seat. "It's kind of damp in this theater," she said. "Very bad for my sinuses. Hope I don't get one of my attacks."

I pretended I was totally into the commercials on the screen.

Jackson had his head down, like he was studying his popcorn bucket.

"Yo, dude," Artie said. He is always calling everyone "dude." Girls, too. "Awesome sweater. I saw one just like it at Old Navy."

Artie grabbed Jackson's sleeve to feel the sweater.

Jackson let out a startled cry as Artie bumped the bucket from his hand. And a ton of butter-soaked popcorn came spilling out.

"My sweater!" Jackson shouted. He frantically tried to brush the popcorn off. But he had two huge butter stains on the front. "My new sweater! I don't believe it!"

I guess I was *wrong* about stains not showing on black sweaters.

Artie shrugged. "No biggie," he said. "It doesn't look too bad." He brushed some popcorn kernels off Jackson's sleeve.

"It's totally ruined!" Jackson said.

"It'll come right out in the wash," Artie said.

He wiped his runny nose on the back of his hand. Then he dug into the bottom of the bucket, pulled out a handful of Jackson's popcorn, and shoved it into his mouth.

Jackson may be the calm one in our family. But you can push him too far.

And that was too far!

Jackson let out a roar. He wrapped an arm around Artie's neck and began wrestling with him.

The popcorn bucket rolled into the aisle, and a little girl tripped over it. She fell onto her knees and started to scream.

Jackson pulled Artie out of his seat. The two of them tumbled into the aisle, wrestling, grabbing at each other, punching.

Nina jumped to her feet and started shrieking. "Don't hurt him! Don't hurt him! You'll *kill* him!"

Up on the screen, a little mouse was telling everyone to turn off their cell phones and be "quiet as a mouse" during the movie.

A skinny middle-aged man in a black suit appeared from out of nowhere. He had some kind of badge hanging around his neck. He grabbed Jackson with one hand and Artie with the other.

"I'm the manager," he said. "You four — let's go. Quickly. You're out of here. All of you — you're under arrest!"

He herded us up the aisle to the exit. People stared as we walked past.

Behind us, I could hear the Butt-Kicker theme song. The movie was starting. But we wouldn't see it.

The manager pushed us through the lobby and out into the mall.

"You're not really arresting us," I said. I couldn't help it. My voice was kind of shaky.

"No," he replied. "I just said that to get your attention. But you're out of here. I can't have fistfights in my movie theater."

He gave us a nasty stare. Then he turned and stomped back into the theater.

Jackson tugged at his sweater sleeve. The sweater was totally stretched out and stained.

We took a few steps into the mall. I just wanted to get away from the Lerner twins. But, of course, they followed us.

"No biggie," Artie said, wiping his nose with

the back of his hand. "I hate superhero movies, anyway."

"Yeah," Nina agreed. "They're too noisy. They always give me a migraine."

I'd like to give her a migraine! I thought. *Why do we always get stuck with these losers?*

"Want to hang out or something?" Artie asked. "Maybe we could get some cinnamon buns over there."

"Yuck. Those are too sweet," Nina whined. "They make my teeth hurt."

"Sorry. We've got to go," I said. I didn't bother to make an excuse. I just pulled Jackson away.

I tugged him past a frozen yogurt store and a Make-Your-Own Panda Bear shop. When the Lerner twins were out of sight, I let go. I slumped against a store window and sighed.

"I was looking forward to that movie for a month," Jackson groaned. "And that jerk Artie ruined it."

I pulled out my cell phone and checked the time. "What are we going to do? We have two hours to kill before Mom and Dad come to pick us up."

"Hey, we're at the mall," Jackson said. "How hard is it to kill time?"

Jackson and I started to walk. He stopped in front of the video game store and stared at some kind of battle game for awhile. I went next door to check out some tennis rackets.

We walked the whole first floor. Then we sat down and had cinnamon buns. "Too sweet," Jackson said. He had icing smeared on his chin.

I finished mine in three bites. "*Way* too sweet!" I agreed. We both laughed.

"Know what I'd do if I was a superhero?" Jackson asked. He was gazing into a travel store with a snowy skiing photo in the window. "I'd pick up both of those wimpy Lerner kids. I'd fly them to the North Pole and leave them on an ice floe with a hungry polar bear."

I shook my head. "Too good for them," I said. "I'd use mind control powers and give them the brains of one-year-olds." I laughed. "Miss Hawking would have to change their diapers in class!"

We both laughed like lunatics. Jackson and I even have the same cackling laugh.

A short while later, we walked outside to where we always meet Mom and Dad. The parking lot was wet, filled with puddles. It must have rained while we were inside the mall.

Suddenly, Jackson gave me a hard shove — and screamed, "Jillian — LOOK OUT!"

I let out a cry as a wave of icy water splashed over me.

I staggered back. Grabbed on to my brother. We both frantically shook water off. We were drenched!

Wiping water from my eyes, I saw a big blue SUV roaring past. The huge car had sent a wave of rainwater over us.

And as the car rolled past, I saw Nina and Artie in the backseat. They were shrugging and mouthing the word *sorry* over and over again out the window.

I hugged myself. I was shivering. "I really hate those kids," I muttered through gritted teeth.

"None of our friends can stand them, either," Jackson said. He studied his new sweater. Totally soaked and ruined.

He sighed. "I can't believe they invited us to their birthday party."

"I can't believe Mom and Dad are making us *go*!" I replied.

I glanced around. Stores were closing. There were just a few cars left in the big lot, glistening with raindrops under the tall lights. "Where are Mom and Dad? They're late."

"Probably watching a ball game and forgot about us," Jackson muttered.

Mom and Dad are White Sox freaks.

I wiped water off my forehead with my hand. Something caught my eye near the mall entrance. A small booth bathed in a purple glow.

"Check that out," I said.

Jackson followed me as I turned and walked over to it. "Cool!" he said. He read the sign above the little booth out loud: 'Madame Doom.'

A fortune-teller's booth. It looked like the ticket taker's booth at the movie theater. The front was glass with a small window cut out of it. It was glass on three sides and it had no roof. Red and purple lights blinked on and off all around it.

Behind the glass, a wooden figure sat in front of a red curtain. An old fortune-teller. She was dressed in purple with a long purple scarf over her black wig.

Her cheeks were bright red. Her eyes were black. The paint was cracked and one eyebrow was chipped away. She leaned toward the glass. It looked as if she was staring right at us.

"Awesome," I said. "Let's find out our fortunes. Where do you put the money?"

We searched till we found a slot on the side of the booth. Jackson found a quarter in his pocket. He slipped it into the slot.

I heard a creaking sound. Slowly, the wooden figure began to move.

Madame Doom blinked her eyes. Her head rolled back, then forward. One pink hand lowered heavily to her side. With a loud *click*, a small white card slid into the hand. Then slowly . . . very slowly . . . creaking loudly . . . she raised the card to us.

I stuck my hand into the opening in the glass. I stretched my fingers as far as they could go. But I couldn't reach the card.

"Her hand is stuck," I said. "It won't come up all the way."

Jackson shoved me out of the way. "Let me try."

He leaned into the booth. He stretched . . . stretched . . . reaching as far down as he could. I put my hands on his shoulders and gave him a little push.

And . . . *ZZZZZZZZZZZAAAAAAAAP!*

We both opened our mouths in shrill screams.

My whole body shook and danced as a powerful shock stung me. Jolted me hard. And sent pain shooting out over my arms and legs.

My eyes shut. I bit my tongue.

Jackson and I fell to our knees. The electric shock had stopped. But my whole body tingled in pain.

I clenched my fists. I took breath after breath. I opened my eyes — and saw the little white card flutter to the ground.

I climbed shakily to my feet. My heart was still pounding wildly.

"Are you okay?" I asked my brother.

Jackson nodded. He stood up and stretched his arms over his head. "Wow. That was a bad shock," he said. "But I'm okay."

My hand trembled as I picked up the card.

"Jillian, read it," Jackson said. "What does it say?"

I had to hold the card between both hands to stop it from shaking. The words on it were in tiny black letters.

I read it to myself. Then I read it out loud to Jackson: "'Welcome to Horrorland.'"

5

"Huh?"

I handed the card to him. He stared at it. Then he looked at me. "HorrorLand? What is that? An amusement park or something?"

I shrugged. "Beats me. What a loser fortune."

A horn honked. I turned to see our car. Dad waved from behind the wheel.

I still felt shaky as I climbed into the backseat. Tingly all over.

"How was the movie?" Dad asked.

"Awesome," Jackson said. "I can't wait to see it *again*!"

The next morning, I beat Jackson down to breakfast. We have a race every morning. First one into the kitchen gets ten points.

I don't know why we do it. Jackson *hates* to wake up. So far, I've won every morning. I think the score is about ten thousand to nothing.

I said good morning to Mom and Dad and dropped into my seat at the kitchen table. "Here's a surprise," Mom said. She set a plate of waffles down in front of me.

I blinked. "I *knew* you were going to make waffles," I said. We usually just have toast or a Pop-Tart.

"You smelled them?" Mom asked, pouring herself a cup of coffee.

"No," I said. "I really knew it. Like a premonition or something."

Rubbing the sleep from his eyes, Jackson staggered up to the table. He yawned loudly right in my face. He thinks that's funny.

"I got ten points — again," I said.

He slumped into his chair at the other end of the table. I gazed down at the steaming-hot waffles and sniffed. I love the smell of waffles in the morning.

"Jackson, would you pass the syrup?" I asked.

I heard a soft *zzzip*, and when I looked up from the waffles, the syrup bottle was right in front of me.

"How did you get it to me so fast? Did you *throw* it?" I asked.

Jackson had the strangest look on his face. He stared at the syrup bottle as if he'd never seen one before.

Mom set Jackson's waffles in front of him. He

reached for his fork — and bumped it off the table. It clattered onto the kitchen floor.

"What a klutz," I muttered. I blinked. The fork was back on the table.

My mouth dropped open. "Am I seeing things?" I asked him.

He stared at the fork. "Weird," he muttered. He shoveled a whole waffle into his mouth.

Dad was frowning as he read the newspaper.

"Do you really think they might shut down the car factory?" I asked.

He finished reading something, then turned to me. "Jillian, how did you know I was reading about the car factory?"

"I — I don't know," I stammered.

I turned to Mom. "If you can't pick me up after school, it's no problem," I said. "I can take the bus."

She set her coffee cup down. "How did you know I was thinking about that?"

Mom and Dad both stared at me. "Are you reading our minds?" Mom asked.

I laughed. "Maybe I am. . . ."

Then I looked across the table — and gasped. One of Jackson's waffles was floating in midair!

"How did you do that?" I asked my brother later.
We were sitting in the backseat of the car, waiting for Dad. "How did you make that waffle
float?"

Jackson had a stunned look on his face. "I — I
can't explain it," he stammered. "I stared at the
waffle, and . . ." He lowered his voice to a frightened whisper. "Jillian, something *weird* is going
on. I —"

Dad climbed in behind the wheel. Jackson
changed the subject. He started talking about
the White Sox.

I tuned out. I thought about breakfast.
Something just wasn't right.

At noon, I stepped into the lunch line at school. I
called to Marci and Ana Li, my friends from the
swim team, to save me a seat.

And guess who jumped into the line ahead of
me. Yes, it was Nina Lerner.

"You don't mind if I get in front of you, do you?" Nina asked. "I have low blood sugar. I have to eat something right away."

"No problem," I muttered.

She picked up a soup bowl, started to raise the lid on the big soup pot, and then put it down. "The soup is probably too spicy. It will upset my stomach."

"No, it won't," I said. "It's just chicken soup. It's not spicy at all."

Nina spun around. Her mouth dropped open. "Excuse me? Jillian, I didn't say anything about the soup."

"I — I heard you —" I said.

Nina squinted hard at me. "I love that skirt and vest," she said.

"I got them at this awesome shop at the mall," I told her. "You know. The one next to Dogs 'n' Things."

The soup bowl fell out of her hand and crashed into pieces on the floor. "Are you a *witch* or something?" Nina cried. "Are you reading my *thoughts*? I didn't say a *word* to you, Jillian!"

She spun away from me and carried her tray down the line.

I stood there, staring after her, feeling strange. I had a whistling sound in my head. No. More like whispering. Dozens of soft voices . . .

"Wish I could have that dessert," I heard Nina

say. "But it might have corn syrup, and I'm allergic."

I gasped. I realized Nina didn't say that out loud. She was too far away for me to hear her.

What's happening to me? I asked myself. *I really AM reading her thoughts!*

I heard a scream from the other side of the lunchroom. I turned around — and let out a cry.

A chair floated in midair above a table.

Jackson sat at the table with a couple of his friends. The three of them stared up at the floating chair. Kids screamed and pointed.

My brother had the strangest expression on his face. The others were crying out in shock. But Jackson looked like he was thinking hard. Concentrating on the chair.

Was Jackson making the chair float?

I remembered the floating waffle that morning.

I had to talk to my brother. We had to figure out what was going on.

Two teachers hurried across the room. One of them grabbed the chair and pushed it back down to the floor.

"I've seen that trick on TV!" a girl said.

Did she say it — or did I read her thoughts?

I suddenly felt dizzy. Confused. I pressed my hands against my forehead.

The bell rang. I set my tray down and hurried to class. I didn't have any lunch. But I wasn't hungry. My stomach felt tight as a knot. I couldn't shake off my dizziness.

On my way to Miss Hawking's class, Brandon Meadows, a friend of Jackson's, passed by me. He gave me a shy wave. And I heard him say, "Wow. Jillian is looking totally *hot* today."

I could feel my face grow warm. I knew Brandon didn't say it. He was only *thinking* it. I read his mind!

"I never knew he liked me," I muttered.

I was desperate to talk to Jackson about what was happening. But class had already started. He sat on the other end of the row from me.

Miss Hawking was telling everyone to settle down.

I waved at Jackson and tried to get his attention. But he had his head buried in one of his textbooks.

I read his thoughts. He was bummed because he did the wrong science pages last night. He hoped he wouldn't be called on.

Could Jackson read MY thoughts? I was desperate to ask him.

Miss Hawking finally got everyone quiet. "I hope you all did your homework," she said. "At two-thirty, I'm giving a surprise quiz on it."

I glanced at the wall clock. It read 2:05.

I turned to my brother. He had a sick look on his face. I could hear what he was thinking: *I'm totally doomed.*

"Take out your wildlife notebooks," Miss Hawking said. "Let's see what you were able to find out about the manatee. We'll start with you, Ana Li. Is it a fish or a mammal?"

I didn't hear Ana Li's answer. I was scrambling in my backpack to find my notebook. Where *was* it?

I pawed through everything. Then I remembered that Nina had borrowed it. And she'd never returned it.

I hoped I could fake it. Miss Hawking gets very angry if we forget our notebooks. I glanced at the clock. Still 2:05?

"Now, tell me," Miss Hawking continued. "In what kind of waters can we find the manatee? Nina?"

I didn't listen to Nina's answer. I turned and gazed down the row to my brother. He wasn't listening to the manatee discussion, either.

He was staring hard at the clock.

2:05.

Jackson didn't move a muscle. Didn't blink.

I tried to read his thoughts. But I couldn't.

Why was he concentrating so hard?

What on earth was he *doing*?

7

"What other sea creatures are related to the manatee?" Miss Hawking asked.

The discussion had lasted at least half an hour.

But the clock still read 2:05. The hands hadn't moved.

Didn't anyone else notice?

I kept my eyes on Jackson. He concentrated . . . concentrated . . .

I knew what he was doing. I knew he had stopped the clock so it wouldn't be two-thirty.

I tried to listen to the science discussion. Miss Hawking asked a question. "Sea lions and walruses," I said. "In the Arctic."

"Jillian, wait till I ask the question," she scolded me.

I could feel myself blushing. Kids were staring at me.

"How did you know what I was going to ask?" Miss Hawking demanded.

I shrugged. "Just took a guess," I said.

Now more kids laughed at me.

I jumped as the final bell rang.

"Oh, good heavens!" Miss Hawking exclaimed. She glanced up at the wall clock. "The clock must have stopped. How did you all get so lucky? No quiz today. See you tomorrow!"

Kids cheered. A few touched knuckles. Everyone packed up and started for the door.

I ran over to Jackson. He was sweating. From all the hard concentrating, I guessed. He had a grin on his face.

"*You* did that — right?" I whispered. "You stopped the clock?"

He laughed. "Yeah. I did."

"And you made the chair float in the lunchroom?"

"Yeah, it was easy," Jackson whispered. "And before I came to class, I closed my locker just by *thinking* I wanted it closed. Believe it? It's totally awesome!"

"I can read thoughts," I told him. "For real. I can read your thoughts."

His smile faded. "No joke? What am I thinking about?"

"A Snickers bar," I said.

He staggered back. "Oh, wow, Jillian. You're right. You really can read minds!"

We walked down the hall toward the front doors. "How did this happen to us?" I asked.

27

He thought hard. "The fortune-teller?" he said. "The electrical shock we got from her booth?"

"I'm kind of scared," I said. "I feel so different. It's fun. But what's going to happen to us? Are we like superheroes now, Jackson? Or are we *total freaks*?"

The next day, we had a soccer game in gym class. Mr. Bennett is our gym teacher. Everyone calls him Coach B.

Coach B is young and tall and very hot. The girls in school all have crushes on him.

We gathered around him as he started to choose up sides. But Artie interrupted. "I can't play," Artie whined, rubbing the back of his neck. "I have a runny nose and a stiff neck. Think I'd better sit this one out."

Good, I thought. *He and his sister are both total klutzes.*

Artie may be the worst soccer player in history. He's afraid to kick the ball. Afraid he might sprain his toes.

"Everyone plays," Coach B told him.

"But my neck —" Artie said.

"Get some exercise," Coach B said. "It'll loosen you up. Your neck will feel better."

Grumbling and rubbing his neck, Artie trotted

across the grass to join his team. I saw that one of his sneakers was untied.

I was on the red team. Jackson was on the blue.

It was a sunny, hot day. The grass on the soccer field shimmered under the bright sunlight. We all played hard and had fun. It felt good to run during the middle of the day.

With about ten minutes left in gym class, the game was tied 2 to 2. I moved the ball toward the goal.

I could read the defender's mind. I knew she was going to zig left — so I zagged right. She spun around, startled, as I sped past her.

Was that cheating? I don't know.

I shouldn't have thought about it. I made a mistake. I passed the ball in Artie's direction.

He stumbled over the ball — fell over it — and hit the ground with a loud *"Oof!"*

The ball squirted out right in front of a blue team player. He moved it down the field — and kicked a goal.

Now we were losing 2 to 3.

Only a few minutes left in class. I saw Coach B checking his watch.

Our last chance to score — but Artie had the ball. He dribbled it between his feet for a few steps. Then he pulled back his leg and gave it a hard kick.

It was a powerful kick — in the wrong direction.

"Look out!" I shouted.

Too late. The ball crashed into Jackson's stomach.

He opened his mouth in a sick groan. His face turned purple, and his eyes nearly goggled out of his head.

Jackson grabbed his stomach and dropped to his knees, gasping and choking.

"Oops. Sorry," Artie called.

Coach B ran over to check Jackson out. But Jackson climbed to his feet and waved the teacher away. His face was still red, but he was breathing normally again.

"Uh-oh," I murmured. I could read my brother's thoughts. And they were all anger . . . anger . . . ANGER. He was desperate to pay Artie back.

The game had stopped while everyone watched Jackson. The ball lay on the grass at the near sideline.

I saw Jackson scowl at Artie. And then he lowered his eyes to the soccer ball and stared hard at it.

"No!" I shouted. "Don't do it, Jackson!"

I went running toward him. Too late.

I couldn't stop him. He sent the ball *rocketing* toward Artie's head!

9

Artie didn't see it coming.

He bent down to tie his sneaker.

The ball sailed over his head and bounced in the grass.

I stepped up beside my brother. He was breathing hard. His forehead was drenched with sweat. But his anger was fading. "Jackson, that was a close call," I said. "Someone could have seen you."

Luckily, none of the kids noticed, and Coach B had his back turned.

"We've got to be careful with these new powers," I said. "No way could we explain to Coach B what you just did. And we don't want everyone to think we're freaks."

"I'm sorry," Jackson said. Then he grinned. "Sorry I missed that jerk."

Saturday morning, I needed my science notebook. And I remembered that Nina still hadn't returned it.

It was a dark morning with storm clouds moving low in the sky. The air smelled like rain, heavy and thick.

I pulled a hoodie over my T-shirt and started out the front door. "Back in a few minutes!" I shouted to my parents.

Jackson popped his head outside. "Jillian, where are you going?"

"To the Lerners'," I said. "I have to get my science notebook."

"Wait. I'll go with you," Jackson said.

I felt his forehead. "Sure you're feeling okay?"

"Artie got a new Wii," Jackson said. "I want to check it out." He grabbed a jacket and followed me outside. "I've been thinking about what you said, Jilly."

"Don't call me Jilly, Jacky," I said. I poked him hard with my elbow.

"We have to be careful with these new powers," Jackson said.

The newspaper sat at the bottom of the driveway. Jackson squinted hard at it — and it went flying onto the porch.

I laughed. "Yeah. I see you're being very careful," I said.

"Don't want it to get wet," Jackson said.

We started to trot along the sidewalk. It had rained the night before, and our shoes splashed in the puddles. The Lerners lived in a big old house two blocks away.

At the corner, two little boys tossed their bikes onto the grass and started toward a house. "Watch this," Jackson said. He had an evil gleam in his eyes.

I read his mind. "No — don't!" I cried. I grabbed his arm.

But I couldn't stop him. He sent one of the bikes floating up off the grass ... higher ... higher ...

The little boys screamed in shock.

Jackson lowered the bike to the ground.

The boys stared at the bike, both talking excitedly at once.

"Just keep walking," Jackson said. "Don't even look at them."

I shook my head. "I don't believe you," I muttered through my teeth. "Do you really think this is all just a big joke?"

"A superhero has to have some fun," he replied.

"We're *not* superheroes," I said. "We don't know how long these powers will last or anything. We have to be careful, Jackson. We —"

I stopped talking because we had reached the Lerner house. It was a three-story, green stucco house. The shutters were broken in front. The front lawn was tall and filled with weeds.

I rang the bell. After a few seconds, Nina answered. "Oh, hi," she said. "Come in. We're busy planning our birthday party."

Big whoop, I thought.

"I just came for my science notebook," I said.

"Oh. That," Nina said. She led us into the living room. There were big moving cartons everywhere.

"You can see we're still unpacking," Artie said, appearing from the back hallway. "Hope Mom and Dad get it done by the party. Not much room to hang out."

Nina sighed. "We've been here a month. But they just haven't found time. And all the dust makes me sneeze. It's really bad for my sinuses."

"Where are your parents?" I asked, glancing around. I saw a den on the other side of the living room. A big-screen TV was on with some kind of Wii game on the screen.

"Shopping," Nina said. "Getting stuff to make the birthday cake."

"We need a big cake," Artie said. "We invited everyone in class." He wiped his nose with the back of his hand.

"I can't decide what kind," Nina said. "I can't eat chocolate. It gives me a rash. So chocolate is out. Mom wanted to make a coconut cake. But Artie and I *hate* coconut. It gets stuck in our teeth."

"Too bad," I muttered. There was no place to sit down. The couch and chairs were covered with wrapped-up lamps and vases and other stuff.

"We can't stay," I said. "Can I just have my science notebook?"

Nina stared at me. Her face went kind of pale. I read her thoughts. There was a big problem with the notebook.

She disappeared for a few seconds, then returned with her head down. She handed me the notebook. "I'm really sorry," she murmured.

The notebook was soaked. A soggy mess. I couldn't even open it.

"I tripped," Nina said. "It fell in a puddle. I'm really sorry, Jillian. I'm so clumsy."

Yes, you are, I thought. I took really careful notes. I wanted to get an A in science. But now . . .

"Maybe you could dry it in the microwave," Nina said.

Brilliant.

"I've got to go," I said. I spun around, looking for my brother.

I saw him in the den with Artie. They both stood side by side, staring at the TV screen with game controllers in their hands.

"Move it this way, and it moves the fighter's hands," Artie was explaining.

I took a few steps toward the den. "Jackson, we've got to go," I said.

He didn't hear me. He loved Wii games. He and Artie began playing a boxing game. Swinging their fists and dancing around like boxers.

They were punching the air with their fists. And the boxers on the screen followed their moves.

"Unh unh unh." My brother was really into it. He started groaning with each punch that he threw. On the big TV screen, the two boxers were pounding each other.

And then, Artie seemed to stumble. His punch went wide — and he *slammed* his fist into my brother's jaw.

"OWWWWWW!" Jackson howled in pain. He grabbed his jaw and staggered back against the den wall.

"Accident! Accident!" Artie cried, dropping his controller.

I read his mind. It really was an accident.

But Jackson let out an angry growl, like an animal. Rubbing his jaw, he moved toward Artie.

I read my brother's thoughts. *Enough is enough.* That's what he was thinking.

And then he thought: *Help me out, Jillian. Let's teach these Lerner twins a lesson.*

I gazed at my sopping-wet notebook. And I began to feel as angry as Jackson. "Okay," I said out loud. "Let's *do* it!"

10

Nina moved beside Artie. Was she trying to protect him?

Jackson narrowed his eyes and stared at them both, concentrating . . . concentrating his powers.

I stared at them, too.

"Hey," Nina shouted. Her eyes moved from me to Jackson. "Are you both freaking out? Why are you *looking* at us like that? What are you DOING?"

"Stop it!" Artie cried. "Stop staring at us like that! Are you *crazy*?"

"You're giving me a migraine!" Nina said. She started to rub her temples.

But suddenly, her hands dropped to her sides. She gazed straight ahead, both arms hanging limply.

Both of them froze. Like statues. Their faces went still. They stared straight ahead and didn't blink.

I tried to read their thoughts. But their minds were totally blank.

Jackson laughed. "Awesome! That was so *easy*! Look at 'em! I totally *froze* them!"

A chill went down my back. "They're not thinking or anything," I said. "They've totally shut down."

Jackson pumped a fist in the air. "Yes! Yes!"

I grabbed his arm. "Maybe we've gone too far."

He pulled free. "No way, Jillian." He stepped close to Nina and Artie. "Maybe now you two will cut us some slack and stop being such wimpy, obnoxious pests!" he said.

He turned to me. "Think they'll remember this?"

"I don't know," I replied. "I don't know what they'll remember." My voice broke. "I don't like this, Jackson. I don't think we should have done this."

"Okay, okay," he said softly. "You're right. We'll unfreeze them, okay? We've scared them enough." He began to concentrate.

The Lerner twins didn't move. They stared straight ahead.

I had a sick feeling in my stomach. I couldn't even tell if they were breathing!

"Hurry up," I said. "Concentrate harder. This is too creepy."

My whole body tingled with fright. Why

did we do this to these two kids? We hadn't even practiced our powers yet. We didn't know what we could do and what we couldn't.

Jackson squinted at Nina and Artie. He clenched his jaw and concentrated . . . concentrated his powers.

I stared at them, too. Trying to beam myself into their minds. I kept thinking the same words over and over: *Wake up! Wake up! Wake up!*

Jackson let out a long whoosh of air. He shut his eyes. "It — it's not working," he stammered.

The Lerner twins didn't move.

"Keep trying," I said. "Please, Jackson — do it! Do it!"

We both concentrated on them again. I gritted my teeth so hard, my jaw ached.

But no. No change.

I stepped up to Nina and shouted in her ear. "WAKE UP! Do you hear me? WAKE UP!"

No. She didn't blink. Not a muscle moved.

Jackson and I grabbed the twins and shook them. We shook them hard, shouting for them to wake up and snap out of it.

Nothing. Nothing worked.

I staggered back, choked with panic. "What are we going to DO?" My voice came out in a terrified whisper. "Jackson — what —?"

I didn't finish. I heard a door slam. The sound made me jump.

"We're home!" a cheerful voice called.

I gasped. I stared in frozen horror at my brother.

The twins' parents were back.

11

Panic rolled over me. I struggled to breathe.

The Lerner twins stared blankly straight ahead. They didn't move.

Their parents would be in the room in a few seconds.

I grabbed Jackson's arm. "Hurry!" I cried in a harsh whisper. "You've *got* to wake them up!"

He stepped up close to Nina and Artie. He squinted hard at them. He concentrated so hard, his face turned bright red.

I didn't know if my powers could help. But I concentrated, too. *Wake up! Wake UP!*

I uttered a cry as they started to move.

Artie let out a groan. His shoulders slumped. He blinked his eyes and took a staggering step forward.

Nina let out a long *whoosh* of air, like a balloon deflating. Her head rolled around on her shoulders. She stared at me as if she didn't recognize me. "Jillian? When did *you* get here?"

I was so happy, my legs were trembling. My heart pounded like a bass drum.

"Jackson — you did it!" I cried.

"Did *what*?" Nina demanded.

Artie stared at the TV screen. Then he turned to Jackson. "Did we finish our boxing match?"

"Uh . . . yeah," Jackson said. "You won. You knocked me out."

Their mom called from the back of the house. "Artie? Nina? Come here and check out the birthday decorations we found at the mall."

"We've got to go," I said breathlessly. I grabbed Jackson and pulled him to the front door.

Nina frowned at me. "Don't you want to see the decorations?"

"No," I said. "I want it to be a surprise. Bye. Catch you guys later."

They stared at my brother and me as we ran out the door. I left the soggy science notebook behind, but I didn't care.

We were out of there. And the Lerner twins were no longer the Living Dead, or whatever we did to them.

It had begun to rain, and it was coming down pretty hard. I raised my face to the sky. The cold raindrops felt soothing on my hot forehead.

Jackson and I started to run, splashing up puddles. "That was close," I said. "Too close."

"We have to practice," Jackson said. "We don't really know our powers. We have to figure out what we can do and what we can't do."

We ran under some trees. Rain washed down on us like a waterfall.

"Should we tell Mom and Dad?" I asked.

Jackson shook his head. "We'd better keep it a secret."

"Mom and Dad have that dinner party tomorrow night," I said. "We could check out our powers then."

"Tomorrow night," Jackson repeated. "Yes. Tomorrow night. We'll do it!"

12

The next night, Jackson and I ate frozen pizza for dinner. Mom and Dad were in their room, getting dressed for the dinner party.

Jackson leaned across the table and whispered to me, "I've been trying to think up a good super-hero name for myself."

I laughed. "How about the Tomato Sauce Mutant?" I whispered.

He squinted at me. "Huh?"

"You've got tomato sauce all over your face," I said.

He growled at me. "Your name can be Fantastic Funny Woman. Ha-ha." He plucked a piece of pepperoni off his pizza slice and flicked it at me.

It landed on my lap. I picked it up and started to toss it back at him. But Dad walked into the kitchen. "What are you two talking about?" he asked.

Jackson and I both answered at the same time.

"Pizza," I said.

"Superheroes," Jackson said.

Dad squinted at us. He adjusted his tie. He hates ties.

"We made up a superhero called the Pizza Surfer," I said, thinking quickly. "Kind of like the Silver Surfer. Only he travels on a giant pizza."

I know, I know. Very lame.

But Dad wasn't really listening. He was searching for his car keys.

I spotted them first. They had fallen onto the floor beneath the kitchen counter.

Jackson saw them, too. He stared at them and made them float up onto the countertop. "There they are on the counter!" he shouted to Dad.

Dad scratched his head. "Weird. Don't know how I missed them."

A few seconds later, Mom and Dad said good night and headed out to the car. Jackson and I watched them drive away.

Jackson stuffed a whole slice of pizza into his mouth. Then he grabbed his Windbreaker and started to the front door. *"Mmmmph mmmmph. Let's go,"* he said.

We stepped out into the clear, cool night. The rain had finally stopped that afternoon. The ground was still wet and marshy. Puddles glowed from the pale quarter moon hanging low over the trees.

We trotted to the small park on the next block. It was surrounded by tall hedges, so no one passing by could see us. The park had a playground for little kids and a picnic area with tables and benches.

There were tennis courts behind the picnic area. They were surrounded by a high wire fence. The courts were empty because they didn't have lights.

The perfect place to try out our new superpowers.

I tried to open the gate. Then I saw the big silvery padlock and the chain. "It's locked," I said. "We can't go in."

Jackson shoved me out of the way. "No problem for Wonder Warrior!" he exclaimed.

He stared hard at the lock, gritting his teeth. I could see the muscles in his jaw flexing as he concentrated.

The padlock popped open and fell to the ground.

"Way to go, Wonder Warrior!" I cried, slapping Jackson on the back. I wanted to tell him that was the *lamest* superhero name I'd ever heard. But it didn't seem like the right time.

I swung the gate open, and we stepped onto the court. I carefully latched the gate behind us and gazed around. Someone had taken the nets down, so there was plenty of room to run around.

"I'm kind of *psyched*," I said.

"Me, too," Jackson replied. "Know what I want to do first? I want to see if we can fly."

I laughed. "Fly? Really? I never even thought about that!"

"I know we have powers we haven't even thought about," Jackson said. I'd never seen him that intense before. He was always the laid-back, easygoing, "whatever" guy in the family.

"How do we test it?" I said. "Just raise our arms in the air and try to take off?"

We both raised our hands high above our heads. Then we bent our knees and leaped into the air.

Our sneakers thudded right back down to the asphalt court.

"We need to get a running start," Jackson said. He leaned down and put his hands on his knees, like a runner in a track meet. "We can do this, Jillian. I know we can."

We both took off running across the court. Faster . . . faster . . . Our sneakers pounded the asphalt.

As I rocketed over the ground, I raised my arms to the sky. "Yes! YES!" I screamed. "I'm FLYING!"

13

I let out a startled cry as I crashed headfirst into the wire fence.

"NOOOOOO!"

I bounced off the fence and staggered backward, struggling to keep my balance. Pain shot through my body.

Jackson hit the fence with a loud *clannnnng*. He bounced off and tumbled onto his butt.

He kept blinking his eyes. He looked totally stunned.

"Sorry," I said. I shook off the pain and ran over to him. "Sorry. I lost it for a moment. I thought I was flying. But I wasn't."

"Just help me up," Jackson said with a groan.

I pulled him to his feet. His Windbreaker had a long smear of dirt down one sleeve.

"Okay, so we can't fly," Jackson said. "Cross that one off the list."

"What's next?" I asked. "Oh. I know. Superstrength. Maybe we have amazing superstrength." I gazed around the tennis court. "How can we test it?"

Jackson rubbed at the dirt smear on his sleeve. "Let me try to pick you up," he said. "That's a good test."

I gave him a hard shove. "Huh? Why? Because I'm so superheavy? I weigh almost the same as you, Jackson!"

Jackson grinned. "I'll try to pick you up with one hand. Is that good?"

I made a disgusted face. "Well . . . okay."

He stepped toward me. He wrapped his right arm around my waist. And tried to pick me up.

I laughed. "Not happening," I said.

He tried one more time. No way.

"Let me try with two hands," he said. He grabbed me by the waist with both hands and struggled and strained. Finally, he lifted me a couple of inches off the ground for a few seconds.

"Forget superstrength," I said. "Cross that one off the list, too."

Jackson let go of me and took a step back. He totally froze.

"What's your problem?" I asked.

He wasn't looking at me. He was gazing past me. His eyes were wide with surprise.

I spun around — and saw someone standing in the shadows by the fence.

Who was it? How long had he been watching us?

He stepped slowly out of the shadows.

"It's a kid," Jackson whispered.

A boy. He moved slowly across the court.

And as he stepped into the pale light from the moon, Jackson and I both opened our mouths in screams of horror.

14

At first, he looked like a kid. He was short and thin, with pale blond, spiky hair. He wore a dark T-shirt and straight-legged jeans.

He had a kid's body — *but his face was ancient!*

I mean, it was a terrifying old man's face. The skin was tight against his forehead and cheekbones. Thin as paper, and so taut you could see the skull underneath.

He didn't appear to have lips. His mouth hung open in a skeletal grin of jagged, cracked teeth. His eyes were dark and sunk deep into their sagging sockets.

He slowly raised a bony, pale hand and waved it at us.

Jackson and I stepped back. "Who are you?" I managed to cry. "What are you doing here?"

When he finally spoke, his voice came out hoarse and raspy, like wind blowing through dead leaves. "Are you enjoying your new powers?"

"P-powers?" I stammered. "What powers?"

"We were just goofing around," Jackson said. "We don't have any powers."

"My name is Finney," the little guy croaked. "You shouldn't lie to Finney."

"We — we're not lying," Jackson said.

I tried to read the guy's mind. But I couldn't pick up anything.

Was he a kid? Was he an old man? Was he some kind of weird monster?

"The Institute sent me," Finney rasped.

Jackson and I stared at him. *The Institute?*

He reached into his jeans pocket with a bony hand. "They picked up your vibrations at The Institute. So they sent me to get you."

I turned my eyes to the gate. It wasn't that far away. Jackson and I could probably run right past this weird guy. He seemed to move so slowly.

I glanced at Jackson. I read his mind. He was thinking the same thing — make a run for it.

"We don't know anything about vibrations," Jackson said. His voice cracked. I knew he was as scared as I was. He started to edge toward the gate.

"We have to go now," I said. "I think you've made a mistake."

53

"The Institute doesn't make mistakes," Finney whispered. Something crackled deep in his throat. His eyes sank back into their sockets till I could see only black holes in his face.

"Are you enjoying your new powers?" he repeated.

"We really have to go," I said. My legs were trembling. But I started to move sideways, inching my way to the gate.

Finney pulled something from his jeans pocket. He held it up to the moonlight. A large jewel. It gleamed red in the pale light.

"You have to see the Inspector," he croaked. He raised the jewel higher and it glowed more brightly, sending rays of red light over the dark tennis court.

"You'll like the Inspector. He's very nice."

"N-no," I said. "Jackson and I have to go home now."

But I suddenly realized I couldn't move.

The red light pulsed from the jewel in Finney's hand. The light wrapped around Jackson and me like wisps of fog. Red clouds folding us inside them.

"You'll like the Inspector," Finney repeated. But his voice was even fainter now, and very far away.

I couldn't move. I couldn't see. Only the billowing red light, flowing around me ... over me ... through me ...

54

And then suddenly the light vanished. Everything went dark. I shut my eyes tight. And when I opened them, Jackson and I were no longer on the tennis court.

We were standing in a small room. The room was crammed with lab tables, computer monitors, all kinds of scientific equipment.

We were facing a wide wooden door. And in big black letters, a sign above the door read: THE INSTITUTE.

15

A wave of cold panic swept over me. I turned to my brother. He stared openmouthed at the sign.

"What are we doing here?" he whispered. "How did we get here?"

"I — I don't remember," I replied. "Jackson, I don't like this. I —"

The door swung open. A smiling man in a long white lab coat stepped into the room.

He had tiny, round black eyes and a long bent nose stuck in a large bald head. He wasn't much taller than Jackson and me. His head appeared too big for his body, and his bald scalp glowed like a lightbulb under the bright lights.

He had thick gray eyebrows and a small gray brush of a beard on his chin. When he smiled at us, a gold tooth glowed in the front of his mouth.

He carried a clipboard in one hand. The other hand was buried in his lab coat pocket. His smile faded as he saw the frightened expressions on our faces.

"Don't be afraid," he said softly. His voice was warm and smooth, like a TV announcer. "You won't be harmed here. I'm a scientist. A normal scientist — not a MAD scientist!"

He laughed at his own joke, a dry chuckle.

"Why did you bring us here?" Jackson demanded. "What do you want?"

"How can you *do* this?" I said angrily. "How can you drag people here against their will?"

He didn't answer our questions. His tiny eyes moved from me to my brother.

"Jillian and Jackson," he said, nodding his head. "Twins often have special mind powers. Did you know that some twins even have their own secret language?"

"We saw a thing on TV about that," Jackson said.

"But answer our questions," I said. "Why did you force us to come here? Did that weird guy hypnotize us or something?"

He frowned at me. "Please, Jillian, relax," he said in his soft, smooth voice. "I'm not going to keep you here for long. I'm going to send you back home in a short while — if you cooperate."

"Cooperate? Why should we cooperate with you?" I cried. "That old guy did something to our minds. He —"

"That was Finney, my assistant," he said. "If we pick up unusual brain vibrations at The Institute, we have to send one of our drivers to check it out."

"What are you talking about?" Jackson demanded. "Who *are* you?"

"Please forgive my rudeness," the man said. He rubbed his short, paintbrush beard. "My real name is very hard to pronounce. So everyone calls me Inspector Cranium."

"Excuse me?" I said. "Cranium?"

He nodded. "Cranium means *skull*. Some of my workers gave me the name. It's kind of a joke."

"Ha-ha," I said, rolling my eyes. "Can we go now?"

"Let me tell you what my job is. I do brain research," he said.

He stepped over to a keyboard and typed for a few seconds. A picture of a giant human brain appeared on the wall in front of us.

"See?" he said. "A normal human brain. Some people think it looks like a disgusting blob of meat. But I think it's beautiful." He smiled and his gold tooth flashed again.

I suddenly remembered my new powers. I turned to Inspector Cranium and tried to read his thoughts. But I couldn't. He was blocking me out somehow.

"Sometimes when people have special mind

powers, it's a *good* thing," Inspector Cranium continued. "Take Finney, for instance. Did you know that Finney is a hundred and fourteen years old?"

I gasped. "For real?"

Inspector Cranium nodded. "He uses his special mind powers to keep himself alive. I think that's wonderful — don't you?"

Jackson and I didn't react at all. Could Cranium be telling the truth? Finney certainly *looked* a hundred and fourteen years old!

Cranium's smile faded. "Then sometimes special brain powers can be a *bad* thing," he said. "I'm not saying you two have special powers. But let's just say you do. . . ."

He scribbled something on his clipboard. His tiny eyes almost disappeared as he squinted at what he was writing.

Finally, he turned back to Jackson and me. "If you had special powers, people wouldn't know how to deal with you," he said. "Your friends would treat you as outcasts. It would be a terrible problem for everyone. You would be treated like freaks for the rest of your lives."

I forced a laugh. "Well, it's a good thing Jackson and I don't have any powers," I said.

I glanced at Jackson. I hoped he caught on. "She's right," he said after a few seconds. "We don't have special brain powers."

"Hmpf." Inspector Cranium made a sound

with his lips. He scribbled on his clipboard pad some more.

"Well, that's why I brought you here," he said. "We usually don't make mistakes. But let's give you a few tests and we'll see."

"Tests?" I started.

Inspector Cranium raised one hand. A smile spread over his face. "Don't be nervous. The tests are very simple. And completely painless. I'll have you home in no time."

His smile faded quickly. "I'll have you home in no time," he repeated. *If all goes well.*

16

He turned and walked to the other side of the lab. His shoes clicked loudly on the lab floor. He started turning dials, pushing buttons, and tapping on keyboards.

"Listen to me," I whispered to Jackson. *"No way* we can trust this guy. Don't let him know we have special powers. If he thinks we're normal, he'll let us go home."

"But how can we hide it from him?" Jackson whispered back. "Maybe he *did* pick up our vibrations. Maybe *he* can read minds."

"Just concentrate on one thing," I said. "The whole time. Just think about . . . think about Nina and Artie and how much you hate them."

Jackson nodded. "That's good," he whispered. "I'll just think their names over and over."

"Me, too," I said.

Inspector Cranium came clicking back to us. He carried a set of headphones in each hand. "Put these on," he said. "They're wireless."

I took the headphones from him. I held them in front of me, studying them.

"Go ahead," Inspector Cranium urged. "Don't worry. You'll be fine. It's easy. Put them on."

I shoved them back at him. "Sorry. I don't want to," I said.

His tiny eyes burned into mine. "Put them on," he said softly.

He kept his eyes trained on me. He didn't blink. Didn't move.

I felt a tingling inside my head. A prickly feeling *under* my forehead.

I tried to scratch it away. But the tingling became a dull ache. And then my temples started to throb . . . throb with a blinding pain.

"Put them on," he repeated, "and the pain will go away."

I took a deep breath. And pulled the headphones down over my ears . . .

I didn't hear anything.

I started to think the Lerner twins' names over and over. *Nina . . . Artie . . . Nina . . . Artie . . .*

I glanced at Jackson. He had the headphones in place. I read his mind: *Nina . . . Artie . . . Artie . . . Nina . . .*

I heard a low hum. The hum grew louder, then disappeared. Silence again.

Nina . . . Artie . . .

I looked up. Inspector Cranium was back against the far wall. He was tapping a keyboard and gazing at numbers on a large computer monitor.

Nina ... Artie ...

Across the lab, Inspector Cranium turned some dials. I heard a soft pulsing sound in my ears. A steady pulse.

Beeep beeep beeep ...

The pulsing sound grew louder. Longer. Until it rose and fell like a deafening ambulance siren *inside my head.*

I opened my mouth in a shrill scream of pain.

But I couldn't hear my own scream over the wail of the siren. My head throbbed and vibrated. The sound shook my whole body.

Frantically, I grabbed the headphones with both hands.

I tugged hard. *The headphones were clamped tight to my ears.*

I struggled to slide them off. I pulled with all my strength.

But they stuck tight, and the siren grew even louder.

"Help me! HELP! It HURTS so bad! I can't STAND it!"

17

The siren faded.

I could still hear it echoing in my ears.

All my muscles were tight. My teeth were grinding so hard, my jaw ached.

"You're almost finished." Cranium's voice rose in the headphones. "I'm reading your brain impulses now."

I took several deep, shuddering breaths. I shut my eyes and tried to concentrate. I started to repeat the Lerners' names again.

Nina . . . Artie . . . Nina . . .

I heard a steady pulsing sound again. Just a soft beep.

Nina . . . Artie . . .

Then silence. A deep silence.

I shut my eyes and tried to relax.

A few seconds later, Inspector Cranium stood in front of us. He removed my headphones, then Jackson's. His lips were pursed tightly. He didn't look happy.

"Very surprising," he muttered. He studied us with his tiny bird eyes. He rubbed his beard. "Very surprising."

"Can we go now?" I asked timidly.

"One more simple test," he said. He pushed a button on the wall.

Finney came silently into the room. A living skeleton with a kid's body. His tight skin was pale white under the bright lab lights, and his eyes looked even more sunken.

"Jillian," Inspector Cranium said. "Tell me what Finney is thinking. Go ahead. Concentrate. Listen to his thoughts. Tell me . . ."

I could read Finney's thoughts easily. I didn't need to concentrate.

Finney was thinking about a slice of apple pie with vanilla ice cream.

"What is he thinking about, Jillian?" Inspector Cranium demanded. "Tell me. Read his mind, Jillian. Tell me what he is thinking about. Tell me . . . tell me . . . tell me. . . ."

I shut my eyes and scrunched up my face. I pretended to be thinking hard.

"Uh . . . is he thinking about a new car?" I said finally.

Inspector Cranium let out a long sigh. He rubbed his eyelids with his fingers. Then he handed the headphones to Finney and told him he could wait outside.

Finney hurried away. He was so light, his

shoes didn't make a sound against the hard floor.

"The Institute usually doesn't make mistakes," Inspector Cranium said. He was staring hard at Jackson and me. "We can usually pick up the vibrations. We always find the special brains."

My heart started to pound. What was he going to do next? More tests?

Cranium let out another sigh. "Finney will take you home in the truck," he said.

He reached into his pocket and pulled out two small white cards. He handed one to each of us. "My business card," he said. "In case you ever need me."

I tucked the card into my jeans. *Why would I ever need him?* I thought. *I don't ever want to see him or The Institute again!*

Finney led us to a small panel truck parked in front. The truck had no writing on the sides. It was solid brown. It had a very small satellite dish on the roof.

Jackson and I squeezed into the front beside Finney. I was a little tense. I mean, can a hundred-and-fourteen-year-old drive?

I shut my eyes most of the way. But he drove very slowly and carefully, with both bony hands on top of the wheel.

About twenty minutes later, we were in front of our house. Finney turned to us. His face was like a living skull. His eyes disappeared in darkness.

"The Institute doesn't make mistakes," he rasped.

I grabbed the door handle. The door was locked.

"Are you going to let us out? Cranium said we could go home," I told him.

"Unlock the door," Jackson said.

Air whistled in and out of Finney's throat. "The Institute will be watching."

"Watching?" Jackson said. "You mean — you're going to *spy* on us?"

"The Institute can send out its *own* vibrations," Finney whispered. Then he clicked the door lock.

Jackson and I leaped out of the truck. We didn't look back. We ran inside.

"Mom! Dad!" I shouted.

Not home. Still at their dinner party.

Jackson grabbed a can of Coke from the fridge and downed it in one gulp. "I am totally creeped out!" he said.

"Good old Nina and Artie!" I said. "They helped us fool a brain scientist!"

Jackson and I slapped high fives. "Follow me," I said. We hurried up the stairs to my bedroom. I dropped down in my desk chair in front of my laptop.

"Let's check out The Institute," I said. "Let's see what we can find out."

I did a search for The Institute. Nothing came up.

Next I did a search for Brain Institute. Still nothing.

"Google Inspector Cranium," Jackson said.

I did it.

Nothing. Nothing at all about Inspector Cranium.

"That's totally weird," I muttered.

"Hey, Jillian — check this out!" Jackson cried.

I spun around. He had the business card in his hand. The card that Inspector Cranium had handed to us.

"I don't believe it!" Jackson cried. "I totally don't believe it!"

He held the card up in front of my face.

It read: YOU DIDN'T FOOL ME.

18

Jackson and I decided that this was all too scary. We had to tell Mom and Dad. We knew it wouldn't be easy, but we had to make them believe us about our powers — and about Inspector Cranium.

The next morning, we hurried down to breakfast. Dad was hunched over the newspaper at the kitchen table. Mom stood at the sink, filling the teakettle.

I grabbed an English muffin and stuffed it into the toaster. Jackson poured himself a glass of orange juice.

I took a deep breath. "We have something to tell you," I said.

"You mean like 'good morning'?" Mom said.

"Yeah. Good morning," I said. "Jackson and I — well, it's a long story, and I know you won't believe us. But it's totally true."

"It's kind of scary," Jackson said.

That got their attention.

Dad raised his eyes from the laptop. Mom set the kettle on the stove and turned to us. "Scary? Like *how* scary?"

"Are you in trouble at school?" Dad said.

"No. Nothing like that," I said. "This is different. This is kind of . . . unbelievable."

"Did something happen last night when we were out?" Mom asked.

"We'll tell you all about it," Jackson said. "But you have to promise one thing."

"No promises," Dad said sharply. "No promises till you tell us what it is."

"Okay. Fine," I said. "It's just that . . . well . . ."

"Just spill it," Mom said. She walked up behind Dad and put her hands on his shoulders.

"What's with all the hemming and hawing?" Mom said. "Just tell us what you have to say, Jillian. You know your father and I will always understand."

"Right," I said. "Well . . . okay. Here goes. I . . . uh . . . well . . . Jackson and I . . ."

I stared at Mom and Dad. My breath caught in my throat. I opened my mouth to try again.

But my mind was a complete blank.

I couldn't remember what I wanted to tell them.

I tried to think. I shut my eyes and concentrated.

How could this happen?

Mom and Dad both turned to my brother. "Jackson?"

Jackson nodded. I could see he was thinking hard. He set down the orange juice glass. He cleared his throat.

Dad jumped up from the table. "Will you two stop acting so stupid and tell us what your problem is?"

Jackson and I exchanged horrified glances.

My brain — it was empty. Empty. Empty.

I suddenly felt sick. My stomach heaved. I pressed my hand over my mouth.

I started to shake with panic. What was *wrong* with me? What was wrong with my *brain*?

"S-sorry," I stammered. "I don't remember what it was."

"Sorry," Jackson repeated. He had gone very pale. "I don't remember, either."

"Guess it wasn't very important," Mom said quietly.

"You're both joking, right?" Dad said. "You cooked up this joke together?"

My muffin popped up in the toaster.

"Have your breakfast," Mom said. "Maybe you'll remember what you wanted to tell us."

"Maybe . . ." I said. I didn't feel like eating. My stomach was churning. My head felt heavy, as if a big rock had replaced my brain.

Jackson and I couldn't wait to get out of the

house. We had to talk. We had to figure out why we couldn't remember.

And as soon as Jackson and I headed out the door, our memories returned.

I gasped as it all came back to me. I started to *laugh*. I was so happy I hadn't lost my mind!

Jackson and I both realized what had happened to us.

Cranium. The Institute. Finney said they could send out their own vibrations.

That's what they did. They'd messed with our brains. They'd kept us from telling our story to our parents. They really were spying on us.

"He controlled our minds," I said. "He kept us from remembering. I — I couldn't even speak!"

"I just have one question," Jackson said. "If he has that kind of power . . . what *else* does he plan to do to us?"

19

The next Saturday afternoon, Jackson and I walked to the Lerners' house for their birthday party. It was a cloudy, gray day. Gusty winds sent leaves dancing down the street.

I carried the birthday presents Mom had bought for them. A new Wii game for Artie. A gift card for a clothing shop at the mall for Nina.

As we walked up the driveway, I could hear voices and music from inside the house. Before we knocked on the front door, we leaned over the stoop and peeked in the front window.

"Oh, wow." Jackson groaned. "Look at all the balloons. So babyish. Are they going to have a clown, too?"

I saw big photo blow-ups of Nina and Artie hanging on the living room wall. And a hand-lettered sign above it read: TERRIBLE TWO!

Yuck.

"Come on," I said to my brother. "Let's get this over with."

But he had his eyes half shut. He was concentrating on something through the window.

I grabbed his arm. "Jackson, what are you doing?"

He giggled. "*Shhh*. I'm going to bust all the balloons at once."

"No, you're not," I said. I tugged him away from the window. "We're going to be nice to them — remember? We decided?"

He rolled his eyes. "Nice to them? Why?"

"Because it's their birthday," I said. "Come on. Give them a break."

I knocked on the door. Nina swung it open. "Hi! Come in!" she shouted.

She was wearing a short black skirt and a pink T-shirt that said BIRTHDAY PRINCESS in sparkly letters.

She had earplugs in her ears. She saw me staring at them. "Loud music gives me a headache," she said.

She pulled me into the room. Seven or eight kids from our class were standing around, drinking punch from little paper cups.

Mrs. Lerner stood behind a table with a brush in her hand. "Doesn't anyone want to have their face painted?" she shouted.

Totally embarrassing.

Jackson hurried into the den, where Artie was

playing a Wii tennis game with his cousins, two five-year-old boys. They kept begging him for a turn, but Artie wouldn't give up the racket.

"Everybody dance!" Mrs. Lerner shouted. "Come on! Boogie! Everyone boogie down!"

No one moved. The kids all looked embarrassed. The music was terrible. So bad, even my *parents* wouldn't listen to it.

I moved toward the den. Jackson handed Artie his present.

Artie ripped the paper off and stared at the game. "I already have it," he said. He handed it back to Jackson. "Can you exchange it for something else?"

I could see my brother grit his teeth.

Nina grabbed my arm. She was holding a paper cup of red punch. "Jillian, I love that white sweater," she gushed. "Is it new?"

"Yes," I said, "I —"

She leaned forward, and red punch spilled down the front of my sweater.

"Oh, I'm so clumsy!" Nina cried. "Mom — paper towels! Paper towels!"

Was that spill on purpose? Or was it an accident?

I read Nina's mind. It was an accident. She was just a total klutz.

Mrs. Lerner studied the stain on my sweater. "We need to pour club soda on that," she said. "Jillian, take it off."

"I *can't* take it off!" I cried. "I don't have anything on under it!"

Nina pulled me up to her room. She took the stained sweater and gave me one of her T-shirts to wear. It was pink and said DIVA PRINCESS on the front in sparkly letters.

"Now *we're* twins!" she gushed.

I groaned. I don't think she heard me. She still had the earplugs in.

She pulled me back down to the party. It was karaoke time.

I admit it. I usually like karaoke. It's fun to get up there and sing like a rock star.

But this was as dreary as the rest of the party. The boys didn't join in. They kept making up gross, disgusting words to the songs. And Nina wouldn't sing. She said she had a bad sore throat.

Artie didn't sing, either. He kept whining that the little kids were hogging his Wii game.

So you get the picture. This was not the world's best birthday party.

About two hundred hours later, Jackson came up to me with a grin on his face. "Watch this," he whispered.

"Watch what?" I asked.

"I'm going to make the birthday cake float out the window. You know. To help liven up this party." He turned and stared at the cake.

"No way," I said. I grabbed him and turned

him around. "Remember our promise? Be nice? And — we don't want the whole world to know our secret?"

Jackson growled. He wandered into the other room to watch the little kids play Wii tennis.

Kids started to leave the party as soon as they had their cake. I breathed a long sigh. "We survived it!" I whispered to Jackson. We started for the door.

But Nina blocked the way. "Don't go yet," she said. "Stay till everyone's gone. Artie and I want to tell you something."

"Tell us something?"

She pressed her finger to her lips, like it was a big secret.

Jackson and I were trapped. It took a long time for parents to show up to get their kids. Finally, everyone was gone but Jackson and me.

"What a lovely party," Mrs. Lerner said. "I'll be back in a little bit, kids. I have to go pick up your dad at the airport. Too bad he missed all the fun."

A few seconds later, I heard her car pull away. We were alone with Nina and Artie.

"We want to tell you something," Nina said.

Artie grinned. "Yeah. We have a little surprise."

What kind of surprise? I wondered.

Nina opened her mouth to explain.

A deafening *CRASH* behind me made me jump.

I spun around and saw the front door burst open.

All four of us cried out as Inspector Cranium came roaring in. His white lab coat flew behind him. His bald head was drenched with sweat.

His tiny bird eyes darted around, taking in everyone in the room.

"Did you really think you could fool me?" he boomed. "Did you really think you could keep your powers hidden from me?"

Jackson and I backed up against the wall. My legs were trembling. My heart started to pound.

I saw Nina and Artie back away, too. Their eyes were wide with fright. Artie stumbled and fell over the arm of the couch.

Cranium angrily stormed toward us.

I knew I had to act fast. But I was too frightened to move or think.

Cranium came closer.

Finally, I found my voice. "Jackson and I are sorry," I said. "We didn't mean to fool you. We —"

"Shut up!" Cranium growled, his eyes glowing with fury.

"But we aren't —"

Cranium cut me off. "I told you to keep still!"

he bellowed. He gave me a hard stare — and I felt a sharp electrical jolt, like a slap.

"Ow!" I cried out, and pressed my hand to my burning cheek.

Cranium was inches from me.

I closed my eyes and tried to block him out.

"You know who I am!" he boomed. "You know what I have to do to you. I have to drain your brains!"

20

I waited for the awful shock and the pulsing pain that would rack my brain. Waited . . .

"Huh?" I felt nothing.

I opened my eyes and saw Cranium standing by the couch. He was staring at Nina and Artie.

Nina screamed.

Artie scrambled up from the couch. "Leave us alone!" he cried.

"You don't want them!" I shouted. "Why do you want to frighten *them*?"

"They don't know anything," Jackson said. "They don't know that Jillian and I have powers."

Cranium sneered. "Who *cares* about your puny powers?"

He turned back to the Lerner twins. "You've hidden for too long," he said. "You give me no choice. I have to drain your brains completely."

"D-drain our brains?" Nina stammered.

"This is totally crazy!" Jackson blurted out. "Nina and Artie don't know what you're talking about. Come on — we're *out* of here!" He grabbed Nina's arm to lead her to the door.

But Cranium moved quickly to block the way. He narrowed his eyes at Jackson.

Jackson uttered a cry. His hands flew up as he felt a powerful electrical jolt. He didn't take another step.

"What does that mean? Drain our brains?" Artie whined. His nose was running, but he just let it drip. "Who are you? Why do you want to hurt us? It's our birthday!"

"It won't help to play innocent," Cranium replied. "I received your vibrations. I know the truth about you two."

My mind spun.

Was it *possible*? Did Cranium think Artie and Nina had powers?

"I have no choice," Cranium said. "As an inspector with the Thought Police, I have to do this for the good of the world."

I stared hard at him. "You drain people's brains for the good of the world?"

He nodded. "We can't allow normal people to have powers. Normal people are too weak, too foolish."

I crossed my arms in front of me. "Huh? Is that supposed to make sense?"

"Only the Thought Police can have that

power!" Inspector Cranium bellowed. "We keep order. Don't you ever wonder why you never meet any real superheroes?" he asked. "It's because we get to them first."

"You mean — without you, there would be *real* superheroes in the world?" I asked.

Inspector Cranium scowled at me. "Lots of people have powers. But we make sure they can't use them. There are very few people in this world who know what to do with superpowers. We know who they are . . . and the rest must be done away with. . . ."

The four of us stared at him in terrified silence.

"Enough talk," Cranium growled. He turned to the Lerner twins. "I have to empty out your brains now."

21

He pointed a finger at Nina and Artie. Staring hard, he began waving his hand in circles as he pointed.

Artie let out a groan.

Nina grabbed her head with both hands. "It hurts! It HURTS!" she wailed.

As I watched in horror, I knew what was happening. Cranium was draining their brains . . . draining away all their thoughts.

Beside me, I saw Jackson start to move. He began waving both arms. Whirling them up and down like a windmill.

He stared at Inspector Cranium and pumped his arms hard and fast.

A few seconds later, Inspector Cranium stumbled backward. He grabbed his throat. He started to choke.

Jackson didn't stop. He kept windmilling his arms and staring hard at Cranium.

Cranium made horrible gagging sounds. He

gripped his throat, struggling to breathe. His face turned bright red.

Nina and Artie stood frozen beside the couch. They were both shaking and pale.

"Run!" Jackson shouted. "Hurry — MOVE! I — I can't hold him for long!"

Before we could take a step, Cranium exploded in an animal roar.

Jackson uttered a weak moan — and fell over backward. He landed with a *thud* on his back on the carpet, stunned, gasping for breath.

Rubbing his throat, Cranium let a smile cross his face. "I beat you, kid," he rasped. "Nice try."

He stepped over Jackson. "Your brother is pretty good," he said to me. "But not good enough. Where was I? Oh, yes. I was dealing with your poor, innocent friends."

"No, please — leave them alone!" I stepped back, out of his path —

— and bumped into Nina.

"No problem," Nina whispered. She patted me on the shoulder. Then she turned to face Inspector Cranium.

Cranium's tiny eyes bulged. "Are *you* going to challenge me now, little mouse?" He laughed.

"How about a flying lesson?" Nina cried.

She raised both hands above her head.

Cranium let out a shocked gasp — and floated off the floor.

He kicked his legs and thrashed his arms wildly. But he was helpless.

Nina waved her arms. And he bobbed up to the ceiling like a big helium balloon. And stayed there, his back pressed up against the ceiling.

Nina helped Jackson to his feet. Then she turned to me. "That was a close one," she said.

Artie hurried out from behind the couch. He uttered a relieved laugh. "Look at the dude up there! Air Cranium!"

"Let me down!" Inspector Cranium cried, his voice hoarse. "Let me down! You can't do this to the Thought Police!"

I squinted at Nina. "So you DO have powers!"

She nodded. "I was born with them. I have the same powers as Jackson. Only a lot more powerful." She smiled. "Artie and I were only pretending to be frozen that day you came over."

"That's what we wanted to tell you," Artie said. "Nina and I were born with special powers. But we learned to hide them. We know about the Thought Police. We tried to keep our powers a secret from them.

"Having powers is too dangerous," Artie continued. He glanced up at Cranium, bobbing on the ceiling. "The Thought Police are always out there. Always looking for people who are different.

"Nina and I act like nerdy, klutzy kids so no one will notice us," Artie went on. "We don't want anyone to know the truth."

Nina and Artie Lerner had superpowers?

I was so shocked, I almost forgot about Cranium.

I looked up. He shouted down at me. "Let me down! I'm SERIOUS! You can't keep me up here! Let me down — and I'll go easy on you and your brother. I just want the others!"

Then, before I could answer, Cranium reached down — and grabbed me by the hair!

22

"NOOOO! Let go!" I shrieked.

He tugged hard, and I cried out in pain. I tried to grab his hands and pull them away. But I wasn't strong enough.

Jackson started to windmill his arms again.

Cranium made a gulping sound. Again, he began to gasp and struggle for breath.

Red-faced, he locked his eyes on Jackson. Jackson uttered a cry — and toppled onto his back on the floor. He tried to get up, but Inspector Cranium's powers held him down.

He tightened his grip on my hair and pulled with all his strength.

Pain shot down my head . . . down the back of my neck. He almost lifted me off the floor!

Then I saw Nina standing very stiff and still. Her eyes were narrowed at Cranium's hand. Nina gritted her teeth . . . concentrating hard.

I heard a sick *popping* sound. Then the crackle of bones breaking.

Cranium opened his mouth in a shriek of pain.

I felt his fingers fall away from my hair. I ducked hard and dropped to my knees.

Cranium was screaming and holding his hand in front of him. The hand looked as if it had *exploded*. His fingers were bent and broken and twisted in all angles.

"Too bad! Did you hurt your hand?" Nina shouted.

My head still throbbed. I brushed down my hair and scrambled across the room to Nina. "Thank you," I said breathlessly.

"Let me down — now!" Cranium insisted. "You can't do this to the Thought Police. You'll never get away with it." He waved his broken hand.

"Enough," Nina murmured. She turned to her brother. "We have to lose this guy. Are you thinking what I'm thinking?"

Artie nodded in agreement. "Yes. STAND BACK, everyone!"

"Finney knows that I'm here!" Inspector Cranium shouted from the ceiling. "He'll bring other officers. You won't get away from the Thought Police. I promise you! Your brains will *all* be drained!"

Artie turned to Jackson and me. "Stand out of the way! I'm going to use MY powers now!"

He waved us back. "My powers are a little different from yours," he said.

"Like how?" I asked.

"Well . . . I can move time."

Jackson and I both gasped. "You mean . . ."

"Let me DOWN!" Inspector Cranium boomed. "Let me down now, and I promise I'll drain your brains quickly and painlessly."

I realized Jackson was concentrating on something across the room. I followed his gaze. He was staring at what was left of the birthday cake. Just a big glob of chocolate on the cake plate.

The three of us watched as the hunk of cake floated off the plate . . . flew across the room . . . shot up fast . . . and smashed into Inspector Cranium's angry face.

He sputtered and cursed, rubbing chocolate from his eyes.

Nina, Jackson, and I laughed. But Artie didn't join us.

"Stand back," he said. "Let's see what I can do to solve the Cranium problem."

23

Artie crossed his arms tightly over his chest. He clenched his jaw and shut his eyes. He muttered some words I couldn't make out.

Then he opened his eyes and raised them to Inspector Cranium, bobbing on the ceiling.

"Let me down!" Cranium boomed. "This is your final warning!"

Artie chanted some strange words in a low voice. He kept his stare on Cranium.

"Your last warning!" Cranium repeated. But this time his voice was higher . . . softer. "You kids cannot handle your powers! You must stop this nonsense and let me down!"

Cranium's voice grew even higher.

I gazed up at him. "Oh, my goodness!" I cried out in shock.

Cranium was no longer bald. He had a full head of black wavy hair.

As I stared, his beard disappeared. He was

growing even shorter. His arms and legs shrank into his lab coat.

"He . . . looks a lot younger," I muttered.

"He IS younger," Nina said, close beside me. "It's working. Watch!"

Artie had his eyes wide on Cranium. With his arms still crossed in front of him, he chanted the same words over and over.

Cranium's hands thrashed at his sides. His shoes fell off and thumped to the floor. He kicked the ceiling with his bare feet.

"Let me down! Let me down!" he shouted in a little boy's voice. "Let me DOWN! This isn't fair! This isn't FAIR!"

And then . . . "WAAAAAAAAAAAH! WAA-AAAAAAAAAH!"

Cranium wailed like a baby.

He WAS a baby. A red-faced baby wrapped in a big lab coat, furiously waving his tiny hands and legs.

"WAAAAAH! WAAAAH!"

"It . . . it worked!" Artie gasped, breathing hard. "I sent him back. I turned back time for him. Wow. That was WILD!"

Nina raised both hands. She pointed up at the wailing baby — and swept both hands toward the battered front door.

Still crying at the top of his lungs, Baby Cranium went sailing across the room — and out the open door.

91

We watched from the window as he went flying over the trees, into the distance.

Then we all started laughing and talking at once. We slapped high fives and touched knuckles and did a crazy celebration dance around the living room.

I'd never felt so happy!

"Artie, that was AMAZING!" I cried. "You BOTH are *amazing*!"

Nina nodded. "Yes, we're amazing," she said. "But we're also in trouble." Her grin faded. "Do you really think we can ever be safe from the Thought Police?"

Jackson and I looked for the Lerner twins at school on Monday, but they weren't there. After school, we walked to their house to see how they were doing.

I rang the front doorbell. We waited. Silence inside the house.

I rang the bell again and knocked. Nobody home?

I jumped off the stoop and gazed into the living room window. "Oh, wow! I don't believe this!" I cried. "Jackson — look! It's empty!"

All the furniture was gone. The room was completely bare.

We hurried around to the back and peered into the kitchen. Dark and empty.

"They're gone," I said. "Just disappeared without saying good-bye or anything."

Jackson shook his head. "The Lerners were only here a few months. Guess they have to move around a lot."

I grabbed his shirtsleeve. I read his mind. We were both thinking the same thing.

Will we have to keep moving, too?

We walked to the shoe store on the next block. Dad had given me money to buy new sneakers.

We walked in silence. We were both thinking hard about Nina and Artie . . . and Cranium.

Outside the store, I stopped — and let out a shocked cry. "Jackson — look!"

On the corner, in the middle of the sidewalk, stood a small booth bathed in a purple glow. A fortune-teller's booth.

Madame Doom!

We hurried over to it. The old wooden fortune-teller sat in front of a red curtain. She was dressed in purple with a long purple scarf over her black wig. She leaned toward the glass as if staring out at us.

"Is it the same one?" Jackson asked.

"Yes — look," I said, pointing. "The same eyebrow chipped away."

Jackson blinked. "But how did it get here from the mall? What is it doing on the sidewalk?"

"Maybe it's following us," I said.

"Ha-ha. Very funny, Jillian."

"Put a quarter in," I said. "Let's check out our fortune."

Jackson frowned at me. "Last time, it said something stupid about a theme park."

I gave him a shove. "Go ahead. Try it. Maybe it'll bring us good luck."

Jackson rolled his eyes. "Yeah. For sure." He found a quarter in his pocket. He slipped it into the slot.

Slowly, Madame Doom began to move.

She blinked. Her head rolled back, then forward. One pink hand lowered heavily to her side. With a loud *click*, a small white card slid into the hand. Then slowly ... very slowly ... creaking loudly ... she raised the card to us.

Jackson grabbed the card.

"Read it out loud," I said. "What is our fortune?"

Jackson read it: *"Take good care of your teeth, and they will take care of you."*

He laughed. "How *lame* is that? That's the worst fortune I ever saw!"

"Hey, wait —" I said. I grabbed the little card from him. "There's something on the other side."

I turned it over and we both read the tiny black type together:

WELCOME TO HORRORLAND.

ENTER
HORRORLAND

ADMIT ONE

WHERE NIGHTMARES COME TO LIFE!

THE STORY SO FAR . . .

A group of kids received invitations to be Very Special Guests at a scary theme park called HorrorLand. They came looking for good, creepy fun—but instead, they found real horror.

Frightening villains from their pasts followed them to the park. A park worker—a Horror named Byron—warned them they weren't safe in HorrorLand. He said their lives were in danger. He urged them to escape to another park—Panic Park.

When Jillian and Jackson received their invitation in the mail to be Very Special Guests at HorrorLand, Madame Doom's fortune seemed to be coming true. But they were afraid to go to HorrorLand. Would they accept the invitation or not?

Jillian continues the story. . . .

Why did my brother, Jackson, and I agree to go
to that scary park? We thought long and hard
about it. Then we realized we didn't want to
spend our whole lives running from the Thought
Police. We needed answers: Where did our powers come from? Why do we have these powers?
And did the invitation have something to do with
the strange new powers we had?

We were on a mission. We had to find out. But
as we looked out on the park from our hotel
room in the Stagger Inn, we agreed it could also
be fun.

But where were the other Very Special
Guests?

We asked the Horror at the front desk, a huge
guy with green fur and yellow horns. He
shrugged. "I think they all got eaten alive,"
he said. He licked his lips. "Yum."

Jackson and I laughed. "You're really not going
to tell us where they are?"

"I just did," the Horror replied.

A woman burst up to the desk. "Can you help me?" she asked the Horror. "There's blood pouring from the sink in my bathroom."

The Horror stared at her. "You were expecting *ginger ale*?"

Jackson and I hurried away. "I don't think he wants to be too helpful," I said.

"Just doing his job, I guess," Jackson replied.

We stepped outside onto a wide plaza. It was crowded with kids and families. I saw a row of shops and food carts. A Horror was handing out helium balloons shaped like human skulls.

A blue-furred Horror stood behind a table with a sign that read: SMALL BITES.

"What kind of food are you selling?" I asked.

"It's not food," he said. "Come over here and I'll BITE you!"

Some kids laughed. Jackson and I kept moving.

"Where should we start?" I said.

"Let's check out the Doom Slide," Jackson said. "Some kids at school told me it was awesome."

"But we came here to learn about where our powers come from," I said. "And why Madame Doom gave us those cards welcoming us to HorrorLand."

"Sure," Jackson agreed. "But while we're here, we can have some fun, right? Let's find the Doom Slide."

"What's so cool about it?" I asked.

"These kids said there are a whole bunch of slides. And if you choose the wrong one, you just keep sliding forever."

I rolled my eyes. "Oooh, scary!" I said. "And you believe in the tooth fairy, too — right?"

Jackson didn't answer. Instead, he narrowed his eyes at me and concentrated.

"Hey!" I felt myself float a few inches off the pavement. "Put me down, Jackson! Give me a break!"

He lowered me to the ground. "Okay, okay," I said. "We'll check out the Doom Slide."

I gave Jackson a shove. "We said we're not going to use our new powers. Remember? We don't want people to see that we're weird?"

Jackson shoved me back. "What's the use of *having* them if we don't *use* them?"

"I'm trying to read your mind," I told him. "But I can't. Because I can only read minds that are bigger than an M&M!"

"Remind me to laugh," Jackson said.

We stepped up to a big map of the park. A little yellow square with an arrow read: YOU ARE HERE. (BUT FOR HOW LONG?)

I spotted the Doom Slide on the map. It was just on the other side of the carnival rides.

Jackson and I crossed the plaza. We started to walk toward Wolfsbane Forest. I could hear low growls on the other side of the trees. Then I

101

heard kids shrieking. I couldn't tell if they were afraid or if they were having fun.

"Jillian — stop —" Jackson said suddenly. He grabbed my arm. He pointed back to the plaza.

"Oh, wow," I said. We both stared at a fortune-teller's booth.

"Madame Doom!" Jackson cried.

"How weird," I said. "She's here, too?"

The wooden figure of Madame Doom sat behind a glass window, staring out at us.

"They must have these booths all over the place," Jackson said.

"Maybe," I said. I felt myself drawn to it, as if Madame Doom was pulling me to her.

Jackson and I both stepped up to the booth. It was glass on three sides. It had no roof. It was open on top.

The wooden Madame Doom was chipped and cracked. The paint on her face was faded and peeling. She sat in front of a red curtain.

"Look — the left eyebrow is chipped off," I said, pointing. "Jackson, I swear. It's the same one we saw back home!"

Jackson squinted at the fortune-teller's faded face. "That's way crazy. How can the same one be in both places?"

"Do you have a quarter?" I asked. "I want to see our fortune."

Jackson made a face. "Last time it was some stupid thing about taking care of our teeth."

"Just put a quarter in," I said. "Come on. Do it. You want to get to the Doom Slide, don't you?"

He grumbled some more as he fumbled in his jeans pocket. Finally, he pulled out a quarter and slid it into the slot.

The wooden mannequin creaked to life. The painted eyes blinked. The head rolled back, then forward. The wooden hand dropped down to her side. When it came back into view, it held a small white card.

I pulled the card from between the hard fingers. Raised it to my face and read it.

"Well?" Jackson demanded. "What does it say?"

I held it up to him. The card read: ESCAPE HORRORLAND.

2

Jackson and I stared at the card.

"What does it mean?" I said finally. "We just *got* here."

Jackson shook his head. "We got two cards that said 'Welcome to HorrorLand.' Now a card telling us to leave. I don't get it. It's too weird."

I kept thinking about it as we turned and started walking past Wolfsbane Forest. The sun dipped behind a wide bank of clouds, and long blue shadows stretched in front of us. Without the sun, the breeze grew chilly.

I shivered in my sleeveless top. Should I go back to the room and put on something warmer?

Jackson and I both stopped short when a man jumped in front of us.

Inspector Cranium!

He was in his long white lab coat. His bald head glowed like a lightbulb in the flickering sunlight. A thin smile played over his face, and his gold tooth flashed.

I turned to run. I pulled Jackson after me.

Cranium moved quickly to block our path.

"What are you doing here?" I blurted out. "You — you were a *baby*!"

He scowled at me. "Sometimes babies grow up fast," he said.

"Let us go!" I cried.

"Did you really think you and your puny friends defeated me so easily? Do you really think your little friend is the only one with power over time?" Then he said softly, "Don't you two know why you're here? Don't you even have a clue?"

"Tell us!" I cried.

"Tell us what's going on!" Jackson demanded.

"You made a fool of me and I want my revenge. . . . He promised me my revenge," Cranium said, moving closer.

"Who?" I cried. "Who promised you?"

"We don't understand you!" Jackson said. "Please —"

Inspector Cranium aimed his tiny eyes at me. "This won't take long," he said.

I could feel his stare. I could feel his eyes burrowing into my brain. Like a harsh beam of white light.

"No!" I gasped.

I gave Jackson a push, and the two of us took

off running. I felt strange . . . a little dizzy. But I broke free of Cranium's powerful stare.

We darted past him, into the tall, tangled trees of Wolfsbane Forest.

"Do you really think you can run from me?" he shouted. "I did my job and now I want you to pay!"

Jackson and I were running hard along the twisting path through the trees. The leaves and branches above our heads were so tangled and tight, no sunlight could filter down. It was nearly as dark as night.

I glanced back. I couldn't see Cranium. But I could hear him.

He was panting hard as he ran after us. Close behind. Closer . . .

We made a sharp turn off the path. I pushed tall weeds out of the way as we struggled through thick underbrush. Somewhere nearby, I heard the wolf howls again.

Jackson and I took another sharp turn, trying to lose the terrifying little man. I glanced back — and saw him trotting after us with his head lowered. He leaned forward as he ran, his hands shoved deep in his lab coat pockets.

And again, I could feel his eyes . . . feel his stare, hot against the back of my head. I could feel the white glare burning into my brain, searching my mind.

Breathing hard, Jackson and I broke out from the trees.

And stared at Madame Doom's fortune-telling booth.

"We — we're right back where we started!" I stammered.

Inspector Cranium came trotting after us. Beads of sweat gleamed on his bald head, and he was wheezing loudly from the long run.

He had his eyes trained on me. "It's my turn," he gasped. "I must go into your brains!"

He moved forward. "This won't hurt very much. Really. This won't hurt very much at all."

3

Inspector Cranium lowered his head and stared hard at me as he moved forward. He was like an animal now, stalking his prey.

I stumbled back, too frightened and out of breath to run anymore.

"Jackson —" I murmured. "He's inside my brain. I can feel it. Tingling. Ohhh . . . it hurts . . . the tingling . . . it hurts."

"Me, too," Jackson whispered. "My whole head is *tingling* from the inside. Just like back in his lab."

I wanted to run. But Inspector Cranium held me in his power.

I turned and saw Jackson staring past Cranium. Staring hard at something behind him.

"Jackson?"

He didn't move. He didn't blink.

And then I saw what he was doing.

I saw the Madame Doom mannequin rise up from its glass booth. The heavy wooden figure floated up slowly . . . rising high above the booth walls.

It tipped back and forth in the air. Then it came flying across the plaza.

Cranium didn't see what hit him.

The mannequin dropped hard and fast. It landed headfirst on top of Cranium, and he crumpled to the pavement.

He didn't make a sound.

Did it knock him unconscious?

Jackson and I didn't wait to find out. He grabbed me by the arm, and we took off running again. Our shoes slapped the pavement as we shot through the plaza.

People stared. A Horror shouted to us, warning us not to run.

But we didn't slow down. And we didn't look back.

The Doom Slide came into view up ahead. A tall purple building with a wide, curving ramp in the center.

We ran to the ramp and started to climb.

I grabbed the metal railing on the side and half pulled, half pushed myself toward the top.

My heart was pounding, and my face was drenched with sweat. My legs felt as if they weighed a thousand pounds as we climbed higher and higher.

"Ohhh." A faint cry escaped my lips when I heard heavy footsteps beneath us. I listened hard as I climbed. And heard grunting breaths. Someone was climbing fast.

It had to be Cranium!

My throat ached and my legs throbbed with pain as Jackson and I reached the top. We ran onto a wide, flat terrace.

In front of us stood ten open doorways cut into a high wall. The doorways were as dark as tunnel entrances. Each opening had a slide behind it. Each door was numbered.

"He — he's coming," I stammered to Jackson. "Cranium. He's right behind us."

"Choose a slide," Jackson uttered. His chest heaved up and down. He lowered his hands to his knees, struggling to breathe normally. "Quick — which one? Which one?"

My eyes ran down the line of slide entrances. At the end, I saw a fat, yellow-furred Horror seated on a folding chair.

"Welcome to the Doom Slide," he said, waving toward the openings. "Pick your doom."

I heard Cranium's footsteps on the stairs. Each *thud* made my heart jump.

"Nine slides are normal slides," the Horror said. "One slide is endless. You will slide forever . . . slide to your doom."

Which one? Which one?

I concentrated . . . tried to read the Horror's mind. But I couldn't pick up any thoughts.

Was it because Horrors aren't human?

I heard a sharp, angry cry. Turned to see Cranium burst out of the stairwell. He pointed a finger at us. "You can get away from me — but you can't escape The Menace!"

The Menace? Who was that? Did I know that name?

No time to think about that now. "Come on." I grabbed Jackson's arm and pulled him to Slide Number 4. I dove through the doorway, into total darkness, and dropped onto the slide.

Jackson was right behind me.

We both sat with our legs straight ahead — and started to dive down.

The slide was steep with curve after curve. Like riding a pretzel, I thought.

Hot wind brushed back my hair as I slid down.

I listened for Cranium. But I couldn't hear anything over the rush of wind and the whir of our bodies against the smooth, curving slide.

Down ... down ...

"I — I don't like this!" Jackson cried behind me.

"It's taking forever!" I shouted.

We spun around another curve, curling down sharply into even deeper blackness.

"Jillian —" Jackson's voice trembled. "Jillian — I think we picked the Doom Slide!"

I felt like screaming. I wanted to cry out for help.

The slide bumped hard and curled again. I had my arms crossed tightly in front of me, so tight it was hard to breathe.

The hot wind brushed my face as I dropped through the darkness.

Then I blinked as I saw a flash of bright light up ahead.

Was that sunlight?

Yes. The slide tilted up and I slowed down. Slower . . . Slower . . .

"Hey —" I let out a cry. And came to a sharp stop at the end of the slide.

I lowered my feet to the ground.

"Look out!" Jackson rammed right into me.

We both stumbled to our feet. We were back on solid ground. I blinked hard, waiting for my eyes to adjust to the sunlight.

It took me awhile to realize that Jackson and I

were surrounded by Horrors. They formed a tight circle around us.

"Wh-what do you want?" I stammered. My heart was still racing from the long slide through darkness. And my throat was dry and throbbing.

"Jillian Gerard? Jackson Gerard?" one of the Horrors asked, squinting at us.

My brother and I nodded.

"Come with us," the Horror said.

"Why? Where?" Jackson cried.

The Horror frowned at us. "We cannot have you wandering around on your own — can we?" His dark eyes went cold. "That just wouldn't be safe."

5

The Horrors tightened the circle around us. Their fur smelled sour, like my friend Marci's dog, who always needs a bath. One of the Horrors spit something brown and disgusting onto the pavement at my feet.

"Let's go," he growled. He raised his big paws to my shoulders to start me moving.

I tried to stand in place, but he was too strong. "Where are you taking us?" I demanded.

"Don't get tense," another Horror said. "We're taking you to your friends."

I stared at him. "Friends?"

"To the other Very Special Guests," he said. He pulled a fat brown bug from the fur on his chest and flicked it away. "They are all safe and sound with The Keeper."

They marched us through the crowded plaza. People stopped to stare. They probably wondered why Jackson and I were getting such special treatment.

Or maybe they thought we did something wrong and were in major trouble.

My mind whirred. "Who is The Keeper? Why *shouldn't* the other guests be safe and sound?" I demanded.

"Sometimes things get scary here," a Horror murmured.

"We just got here today," Jackson explained. "We don't know what you're talking about. Really."

"Almost there," a Horror said. He pointed to a building up ahead. It was a redbrick building with a marquee over the wide entrance. The marquee read: HAUNTED THEATER.

"You're taking us to a *show*?" I asked.

No one answered me.

The Horrors began walking faster. Jackson and I had no choice. We had to jog to keep up with them.

A sign in front of the theater read: MONDO THE MAGICAL.

"I'm totally confused," Jackson whispered. "A magic show?"

At the side of the theater, I glimpsed two kids, a boy and a girl. They both had straight black hair and bright blue eyes. They peeked out at us from the corner of the building.

Why were they watching Jackson and me so closely? I just got a quick glance at them. When I turned to stare back, they both ducked quickly out of sight. I don't know why, but just the sight of them made me feel uneasy, suspicious. . . .

The Horrors led Jackson and me to a small gift shop next to the theater. Painted on the front window were the words MONDO'S TRICKS AND TREATS.

We pushed into the store and down a narrow aisle. It was a magic store. The shelves were filled with magic tricks, wands, top hats, and other magician gear.

They marched us through a back room. Then to a stairwell in the far wall.

"Down there," a Horror said. "Watch your step."

The stairway was steep and narrow. Our shoes thudded on the metal steps. The air grew hotter as we climbed down.

One flight . . . two . . .

I took a deep breath. *Stay calm, Jillian. You can handle this.*

But there we were, three flights belowground. If we needed help, no one would ever find us down there.

What did they plan to do with us?

They unlocked a door at the bottom of the stairs. They pushed Jackson and me into a big room.

"The Keeper is waiting for you," a Horror said.

"Keeper?" I asked. My voice cracked.

"Don't make him angry," another Horror said. "He can be . . . harsh."

I didn't like the sound of that.

The Horrors didn't follow us into the room. The door clicked shut behind my brother and me.

Jackson and I took a step into the brightly lit room. A huge room that looked like it had been decorated by a five-year-old!

Furry orange and green chairs and couches. A big zebra-skin rug. Bright yellow wallpaper with blue fish all over it. A purple-and-white polka-dot table with big claws on the legs. A striped floor lamp painted red and white like a barber pole, and overhead, a huge crystal chandelier.

So many colors, it was almost *blinding* down there! It took me a few seconds to see that the room was crowded with kids. They were all about our age. And standing in front of the kids — two men in totally weird superhero costumes.

One of them was dressed in red-and-blue tights, feathery yellow boots, and a leopard-skin cape.

The other man was bigger, broader, with bulging biceps and a wide chest. He was dressed all in purple — purple tights and top, purple cape, purple boots. He had a purple mask pulled halfway down his bright red face.

When I got over my shock, I saw that the purple guy was using both hands to hold a boy off the floor. The boy kicked and struggled, but the superhero wouldn't let him down.

"Let me go! Let me down!" the boy screamed.

Both superheroes suddenly discovered Jackson and me. They turned and stared at us through their masks.

"Do you know what POPS my PETUNIAS?" the purple one screamed. "Fresh meat!"

The guy in the crazy costume tossed his head back and laughed like a hyena. When he finished his insane laughing, he began to chant: "Fresh meat. Fresh meat. Fresh meat. What rhymes with meat? *Eat?* Hahahaha."

The purple one dropped the boy to the floor. The boy hit hard, then scrambled over to the other kids.

Then the purple one began taking long, heavy strides across the room to Jackson and me. "Did you come to see what the Purple Rage can do when he's in a RAGE?" he bellowed. "Well, goody. You're just in time!"

I gazed across the room and quickly read the minds of the other kids.

This is real, I realized. *Not a joke. These kids are truly afraid.*

But — who were these two insane-looking superheroes? And why were we all locked in this room with them?

"Know what PICKLES my PASTRAMI?" the one who called himself the Purple Rage boomed. He pointed to my brother. "YOU!" he cried.

He opened his mouth in a fierce animal roar. "Hear me RAAAAAGE!" he bellowed. "YAA-AAAAIIIIII!"

Then he dove at Jackson with both gloved hands raised, as if to strangle him.

The other kids let out horrified cries.

Jackson acted quickly. He raised his eyes to the ceiling. And as the Purple Rage pounced, Jackson sent the crystal chandelier plunging down on him.

The chandelier crashed onto the superhero's head and shoulders. The Rage uttered a weak cry. He toppled facedown onto the floor.

The chandelier shattered over him, burying him beneath it. Glass splintered and flew everywhere.

Everyone ducked and ran out of the way.

Groaning, the Rage shoved the mangled chandelier off his back. Slowly, very slowly, he pulled himself to his feet. He had shards of glass stuck to his face and the front of his costume.

"That BURSTS my BALONEY!" he screamed at the top of his lungs. He made two giant fists. His eyes goggled. He clenched his teeth. He twisted his face in a furious rage.

"That PARBOILS my PEONIES!" he bellowed. He began pounding his fists against his chest. *THUD THUD THUD.*

"That SPLITS my SPAGHETTI!"

Then he let out another deafening animal roar. And he EXPLODED.

His body burst apart with a loud *SPLAAAAAT.*

I covered my eyes and ducked as his purple guts went flying all over the room.

Kids screamed and dove out of the way.

When I looked up, the floor was puddled in wet gobs of purple and red.

A hush fell over the room. The kids all looked stunned. No one said a word. No one moved.

The other superhero stepped forward. He pushed back his leopard-skin cape. A crooked smile spread over his face.

"My turn!" he shouted. "Did you forget that I was here?"

He shook his head. "That purple punk was asking for trouble. Someone better shovel him up! I hate a messy houseguest — don't you? Hahaha."

No one laughed. I gazed down at the puddles of what had been the Purple Rage.

"Did you forget that I, Dr. Maniac, am your Keeper?" the superhero cried, tossing back his cape. He gazed around the room, his eyes stopping at each kid. "You still have to deal with me, kiddies!"

"You're crazy!" a girl shouted.

"I'm not crazy!" the superhero bellowed. "I'm a MANIAC!"

I turned to Jackson. "This isn't really happening — is it?"

"Maybe this will slow you punks down!" Dr. Maniac declared. "If you can't take the HEAT, stay out of the FURNACE! Hahahahaha!"

He threw a switch on the wall.

We heard a loud hum.

Everyone stood there silently, waiting . . . waiting.

And then some kids started to scream.

At first, I didn't feel it. Then I began to feel the warmth creeping up from my feet.

Waves of heat billowed up from the floor. The air grew hot. I sucked in a deep breath, and my nostrils burned.

The heat rose up from the floor and radiated off the walls.

"Ow!" I cried out. The soles of my shoes stuck to the floor. The burning heat floated from below and wrapped all around me.

Kids began hopping up and down. Shrieking and pleading for Dr. Maniac to shut off the heat. The floor was like a burning griddle.

Sweat ran down my face, down my back. My clothing stuck to my skin.

Jackson's face was bright red, glowing with sweat. He was panting loudly, gasping for breath.

Kids scrambled onto the chairs and couches to

rescue their scalding feet. The air grew hotter, so hot and dry, my skin burned, and my eyes felt scratchy and raw.

"Turn it off! Turn it off!" a girl screamed.

"Can't breathe!"

"I'm . . . burning . . . burning up . . ."

Dr. Maniac kept his yellow-gloved hand on the switch. His wide grin stayed frozen on his face. "Suntan lotion, anyone?" he shouted. "Are you getting a good BURN?" He laughed his ugly laugh.

"Please . . . can't . . . breathe . . ." a boy gasped.

"Ow . . . It burns! It BURNS so bad!"

"Turn it off! Please — turn it off!"

Suddenly, I heard the thoughts of the boy next to me. His dark hair was matted wetly over his forehead. His shirt was drenched. But he stood very still, not wriggling from the heat.

I used my powers to study his mind. His name came to me — Robby Schwartz. The names of the other kids were coming to me, too.

Robby stared at Dr. Maniac, thinking hard.

I created Dr. Maniac, Robby thought. *He's my comic-strip character. I made him up. I know him better than anyone. How can I destroy him? How?*

"I know you kids all like to be COOL!" Dr. Maniac boomed. He threw another switch on the wall. "How cool can you get?" he cried.

The waves of heat faded. I breathed a sigh of relief. My hair was soaked. I wiped sweat off my forehead with one hand.

The room cooled down. We all felt better ... more comfortable.

It didn't last long.

"The temperature is dropping!" a boy named Billy cried. He hugged himself. I could see him shivering.

My breath fogged in front of me. A cold wind caught the back of my neck and sent a chill down my back.

We were still so hot, drenched with sweat. The sudden cold felt as if we had stepped from a blazing-hot beach into a deep freezer.

I began to shiver. My skin prickled from the cold. I couldn't stop my teeth from chattering.

"Careful, everyone!" Dr. Maniac shouted. "Don't catch your DEATHS! Hahahaha!"

Beside me, Robby Schwartz continued to stare at the superhero, thinking hard. He began to shiver. His arms quivered at his sides.

"Help me!" Robby shouted. "Help me! Help me!" His voice came out high and shrill. His whole body trembled from the cold.

"Help me — please!" he pleaded. "I ... I can't take it! I can't take the cold!"

Robby uttered a heavy groan. Then his eyes rolled up in his head. His mouth dropped open. And he collapsed to the frozen floor at my feet.

He didn't move.

Kids screamed in horror.

I bent down. I leaned over him. I turned him onto his back.

A terrified hush fell over the room.

I put my hands on Robby's cold cheeks. I lifted his head gently. Then I set it back down.

I placed my hand on his chest and listened.

Then I raised my eyes to Dr. Maniac. "You KILLED him!" I screamed angrily. "He's DEAD! Robby is DEAD!"

Kids gasped. Some covered their faces or turned away.

I climbed slowly to my feet. I kept my eyes on Dr. Maniac. "You are a murderer!" I shouted. "You killed him!"

Dr. Maniac's grin finally faded. Beneath his orange visor, his eyes went wide. He clapped his hand to his mouth. "No!" he shouted. "No!"

The room grew silent.

I pointed my finger at the superhero. "Murderer!" I said again.

"No! No one can die!" Maniac cried. "I'm The Keeper! My job is to *keep* you here! No one can die!"

He took a step toward me, then stopped. "Is he really dead? Really?"

I nodded.

"I'm ruined!" Dr. Maniac wailed. "Ruined! The Menace will KILL me now!"

The Menace? That's the second time I've heard that name. Who is that?

I quickly read other kids' minds. They were clueless, too. They had never heard of The Menace.

"I'm ruined! I'm MEAT! I'm nothing but contaminated meat now!" Dr. Maniac screamed.

He let out a sob. "No! I can't end this way! I always promised myself a HAPPY ENDING! No! No way! I can't *handle* this!"

He began to scream, howling like a hound dog.

Then he shot his arms forward as if he wanted to take off flying. And he ran right through us. Darted past Robby sprawled on the floor. His leopard-skin cape rustled behind him as he ran by and disappeared from the room.

A few seconds later, I heard the door slam. We could hear his running footsteps clanging up the stairs.

Then silence.

No one moved.

"He's . . . gone," a girl named Carly Beth said. "He left us here."

Robby lifted his head from the floor. "Is he really gone?"

Kids cried out in shock.

Gazing around the room, Robby picked himself up quickly. He brushed off the knees of his jeans.

Kids cheered happily. A few kids rushed forward to hug Robby.

"You're alive! You're okay!"

Robby turned to me. "How did you know?" he asked. "How did you guess my plan to freak out Dr. Maniac?"

"I didn't guess," I told him. "I can read minds. I read your thoughts. I knew you were going to *pretend* to be dead so that maniac would go crazy."

Robby shook his head. "You can read minds? That's awesome!"

"And I can use my mind to make things move," Jackson said. "Maybe I can unlock the door, and we can get out of here!"

We stampeded to the door.

Jackson grabbed the knob. He twisted it. Then he turned to the rest of us.

"I . . . I don't believe it!" he cried.

"It isn't locked," Jackson said. He pulled the door open all the way.

Robby snickered. "Dr. Maniac left in such a panic, he forgot to lock it."

"Let's go!" Carly Beth cried.

"Wait," I said. "Where are we going? Why were you all locked down here with that nutcase superhero? I don't understand any of this."

Matt Daniels stepped up to me. "We are all Very Special Guests," he said. "And we have to get out of HorrorLand. We were brought here for a reason. But we don't know why. We just know there are a lot of evil characters trying to hurt us here."

"We're trying to get to another park," a girl named Julie said. "A place called Panic Park. Three of our friends are already there."

"We'll be safe there," Matt said. "The Horrors in this park are evil. They are all out to get us.

We have to escape HorrorLand and get to Panic Park."

"How? Where do we go?" I asked.

"Follow me," Matt said, starting out the door. "I have a plan. We have to go back to the hotel."

We made our way up the metal stairs. Then we hurried through the magic shop and out into the sunlight.

The Stagger Inn stood on the other side of Zombie Plaza. It seemed like miles away.

We were all too frightened to talk. We walked in single file and kept in the shadows of the shops. Whenever we saw any Horrors, we tried to blend into the crowds and wait for them to pass.

We were hurrying past a mask store when I spotted those two kids again. The same boy and girl with the black hair and blue eyes. They were tall and thin and very pale. They were watching us intently from behind a low brick wall.

Again just the sight of them gave me a chill. Who were they? Were they spies for the Horrors?

We sneaked into the hotel through a back door. Matt led the way down a long hall.

I hurried to catch up to him. "What's your plan?" I asked.

We turned a corner. He didn't slow down. "We have to find mirrors," he said. "Did you notice there aren't any mirrors in HorrorLand? That's because mirrors are the way to escape. We can travel through mirrors to Panic Park."

I shook my head. "I don't understand."

"Britney and Molly are two Very Special Guests who disappeared," he explained. "They were sitting in a café in this hotel. They stepped through the mirrors on the wall. And they ended up in the other park."

Carly Beth moved in front of Matt. "But we already looked for the café," she said. "And we couldn't find it. It disappeared, remember? What makes you think you can find it now?"

Matt pulled a gray card from his jeans pocket. "This is the room key card that Byron gave me." He turned to me. "Byron is the only Horror who is on our side. He's been trying to help us get to Panic Park."

"You're going to use the key card?" Carly Beth asked. "How?"

"I'm not sure," Matt confessed. "Maybe hold it up to the wall or something. It's opened a lot of places for us. It got us into the café before. Maybe it'll help us find that café."

Carly Beth shook her head. "I think we're wasting our time, Matt. The café is gone. Look." She slapped her hand against the wall. "It's solid. There's nothing behind it."

"It's our only chance," Matt argued. He held the gray card up to the wall. He slid it along the wallpaper.

"Come on, wall — move!" he cried. "Come on — *please* — open up!"

10

Nothing happened.

Matt began to walk back and forth, sliding the card along the wall. "Come on, card. Work your magic. Open up the wall!"

Nothing.

He groaned. "I know the café was right in this spot. How could it just disappear like that?" He tried again, sliding the key card over the dark wallpaper.

Jackson pushed through the crowd of kids and stepped up beside us. "Let me try," he said. He narrowed his eyes and began to concentrate on the wall.

"What's he doing?" Robby asked. "Why is he staring like that?"

I opened my mouth to answer. But a loud *CRAAAAACK* made me stop. I jumped back as a jagged crack ran down the wall.

Kids gasped as the crack grew wider and the

wall slowly pulled apart. Jackson stared hard —
and the wall slid open like sliding doors.

"It — it's working!" I cried.

As the wall slid away, a window came into
view. Through the window, I could see a brightly
lit restaurant with blue-and-white checkered
tablecloths on the tables.

Behind the two rows of tables, the walls were
covered in mirrors.

The wall pulled away even more to reveal a
glass door.

"Yes! Yes!" Matt pumped his fists in the
air. He slapped Jackson a high five. "You're a
genius!" he cried.

Matt slid the key card into a slot beside the
door. The door swung open and we burst inside.
No one there.

It seemed to be an ice cream parlor. I saw big
tubs of ice cream in a freezer near the front. A
sign behind the counter read: 550 SICKENING FLA-
VORS! TRY 'EM ALL TODAY!

Matt led the way to the mirror on the back
wall. He stabbed a hand forward — and the hand
disappeared into the mirror.

"The glass is soft — like liquid!" he cried.
"Let's go, everyone! We're outta here!"

"Careful," Carly Beth warned. "One at a time.
Line up. Come on. Into the mirror — one at
a time."

She called off the kids' names as they stepped into the glass and disappeared. . . .

"Billy . . . Sheena . . . Boone . . . Sabrina . . . Abby . . ."

"How weird is this?" Jackson said to me. "They're gone! They walked right into the mirror!"

Before I could answer, an angry voice boomed from behind us: "Are you kids *crazy*? What do you think you're *doing*?"

I spun around as two Monster Police in black-and-orange uniforms burst into the café. They raised long black clubs and came running at us. "What are you doing?" one of them demanded again.

"Escaping," Jackson called to them.

He turned his gaze to the ice cream freezer. The door slid open. And then the big tubs floated into the air. And came crashing down on the two Horrors.

The Monster Police let out angry groans and toppled to the floor under the tubs. Their black clubs went flying.

Then the rest of us — all six of us — dove into the mirror at once.

11

"OWWWW!"

I screamed as my forehead cracked into solid glass.

Beside me, the other kids cried out in shock and pain, and bounced off the glass, staggering back.

Shaking off the pain, I punched the mirror with both fists. The glass was hard. No way to escape into it.

We were all rubbing our foreheads. Robby cupped his hand over a bloody nose. Kids pushed against the glass, but it was no use.

Five kids had made it through. Six of us were left.

And now the bright café began to fade. The blue-and-white-checkered tablecloths dimmed to gray. The lights began to flicker out.

Still dazed, we were standing in the hallway again, staring at a solid wall.

I heard thundering footsteps running toward

us. And from around a corner came four more Monster Police officers waving clubs.

"Run!" Carly Beth screamed.

"Where?" Julie cried.

We turned and charged down the long hall. "To the lake," Matt said. "We can *swim* out of this park if we have to!"

"STOP!" an officer yelled. "Stop! We just want to *talk* to you!"

"Then why are they waving clubs?" Carly Beth asked breathlessly.

We whirled around a corner, down a long hall with the Monster Police close behind. Out a door into the crowded park. Zigzagging through kids and families, trying to lose our pursuers in the crowds.

Jackson and I didn't know where the lake was. We followed the others. I kept glancing back. I didn't see the Monster Police. But I knew they were close behind.

My chest throbbed as we finally reached a round blue lake. No one in the water. I spotted a row of canoes tethered to a short dock.

"Into the canoes," Matt gasped. We were all breathing hard, totally winded.

The canoes tossed and bobbed in the water as we scrambled into them, two to a canoe. Jackson held a canoe steady as I dropped onto the seat. He tossed off the rope holding it to the dock and leaped in behind me.

I began paddling furiously.

Robby and Julie paddled beside us. Matt and Carly Beth shared the third canoe. Matt kept waving us forward. He and Carly Beth pulled ahead to lead the way.

We're doing it, I thought. *We're getting away.*

But does this lake really lead out of the park?

I learned to paddle during a long canoe trip at camp last year. But I'd never paddled so hard and fast before. Leaning forward, I put all my strength into it.

I screamed when I heard the cracking sound beneath me. Jackson screamed, too.

And then I felt cold water seep up my legs. "The bottom!" I cried. "The bottom dropped out of the canoe!"

I slid down fast, unable to catch myself. Into the cold water. I sank below the surface, then raised my arms and pulled myself back up.

Sputtering, swimming in place, I shook water out of my eyes. "Jackson?"

He was swimming beside me. All six of us were in the water, splashing hard, trying to get over our surprise.

"I forgot!" Matt shouted. "Those canoes — they're part of a ride. It's the Bottomless Canoe Ride."

"Now he tells us!" Robby cried.

Everyone laughed. Nervous laughter.

We swam in circles, trying to figure out how

far we had come. Not far enough. We had no choice. We had to return to the dock where we started.

Soaked and shivering, I climbed onto the muddy shore. I turned and helped pull Julie out of the water.

We were all hugging ourselves, shaking off water, our teeth chattering.

"Now what?" Robby asked. "We can't just stand here soaking wet."

I heard voices. I turned to see a boy and girl running toward us. I recognized them instantly. The two kids who had been watching us.

The six of us huddled together.

"You've been spying on us — haven't you!" I cried.

The girl nodded. "Yes, it's true," she said. "We've been watching you."

"Who are you?" I asked. "Why are you spying? Why are you working for the Horrors?"

The boy laughed. "Huh? Us? Working for the Horrors?"

"We're not," the girl replied. "My name is Lizzy Morris. This is my brother, Luke. Luke and I have been to HorrorLand before. We know you're in a lot of danger."

"We know you're trying to escape," her brother said. "But we think you're making a terrible mistake. We think you need to stay here in HorrorLand."

That made everyone angry.

"You're crazy!"

"You really *are* working for the Horrors!"

"*No way* we're staying here!"

"We don't work for the Horrors. We're trying to help you," Lizzy insisted. "We really think you will be safer here in HorrorLand."

Carly Beth glared at them suspiciously. She turned to me. "Jillian, can you read Lizzy's mind? Is she telling the truth?"

I narrowed my eyes at Lizzy and concentrated.

"No," I said. "She's lying."

Lizzy's blue eyes bulged. Her mouth dropped open.

"Don't deny it," I said. "You're lying!"

She and her brother took a step back.

But the six of us quickly surrounded them.

"Why are you *really* here?" Matt demanded. "Tell us! Tell us! What are you trying to *do* to us?"

To be continued in . . .

#11 ESCAPE FROM HORRORLAND

FEAR FILE #10

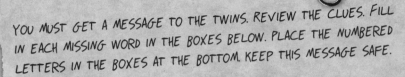

YOU MUST GET A MESSAGE TO THE TWINS. REVIEW THE CLUES. FILL IN EACH MISSING WORD IN THE BOXES BELOW. PLACE THE NUMBERED LETTERS IN THE BOXES AT THE BOTTOM. KEEP THIS MESSAGE SAFE.

1. BRITNEY'S ROOM IS ON THE $\underset{1}{\_}\underset{2}{\_}\_\_\_\underset{3}{\_}\_\_\_\_$ FLOOR.

2. MATT GIVES BILLY A GRAY $\_\_\underset{4}{\_}\_\_\_\_\underset{5}{\_}\_\_\_$.

3. BYRON USES A $\_\_\_\_\_\underset{6}{\_}$ TO CONTAIN THE MONSTER BLOOD.

4. MOLLY AND HER FRIEND RIDE $\_\_\_\;\_\underset{7}{\_}\_\_\_\;\_\_\;\_\_\underset{8}{\_}$.

5. THE $\_\_\_\underset{9}{\_}\_\_\underset{10}{\_}\_\_\_\_\_$ GIVES ROBBY AN ODD FEELING.

6. $\underset{11}{\_}\_\_\_\_'\_$ SPECIAL TOKEN HAS A PYRAMID ON IT.

7. MICHAEL DISCOVERS LUKE AND LIZZY'S $\underset{12}{\_}\;\_\;\underset{13}{\_}\_$.

8. JULIE'S CLUE CONFIRMS THAT THE CAFÉ IS IN $_____\underset{14}{\_}\_$.

9. BOONE LEARNS THE HORRORS ARE $\_\underset{15}{\_}\_\_\_\_$ OF SNAKES.

10. MADAME DOOM GIVES JILLIAN AND JACKSON $\_\_\underset{16}{\_}\_$ CARDS.

GET THIS MESSAGE TO THE TWINS:

| 12 | 8 | 16 | 4 | 6 | 3 | | 1 | 7 | 8 | | 15 | 13 | 14 | 10 | 2 | | 5 | 11 | 14 | 9 |

IMPOSTER ALERT! INTRUDER ALERT!

There is a spy in HorrorLand. If you suspect a spy, ask them these questions. If they get any incorrect, take them immediately to The Keeper.

A mirror is to be:
- A. Polished
- B. Gazed into
- C. Destroyed
- D. Saved for special occasions

The Horror known as Byron is to be:
- A. Treated with the utmost respect
- B. Regarded with suspicion
- C. Watched closely, he knows secret information
- D. Rewarded for his efforts

A visit to Panic Park is:
- A. An excellent treat
- B. A grim event
- C. Only for Very Special Guests
- D. Impossible—no such park exists

TOP SECRET DOCUMENT

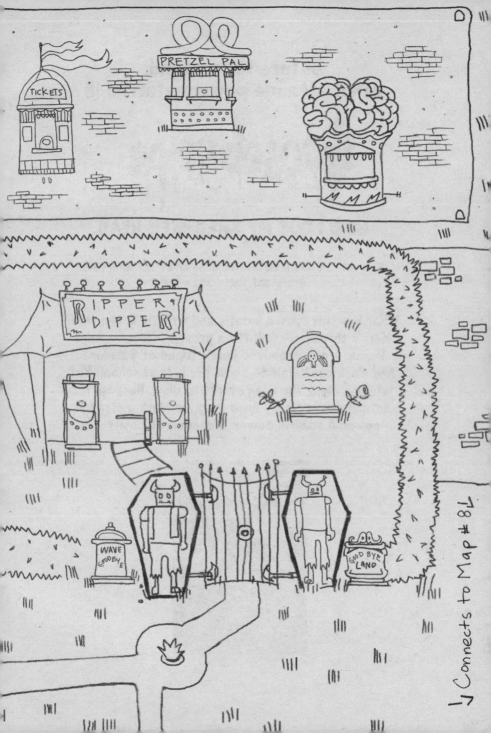

Connects to Map #8L

Before HorrorLand,
other strange powers starred in

HOW I GOT MY SHRUNKEN HEAD

Now with all-new bonuses, including an author interview,
gross-out facts, and more!

What has two eyes, a mouth, and wrinkly green skin?
Mark's shrunken head! It's a present from his Aunt
Benna. A gift from the jungle island of Baladora.
And Mark can't wait to show the kids at school! But
late one night the head starts to glow. Because it's
actually no ordinary head. It gives Mark a strange
power. A magical power. A dangerous power . . .

About the Author

R.L. Stine's books are read all over the world. So far, his books have sold more than 300 million copies, making him one of the most popular children's authors in history. Besides Goosebumps, R.L. Stine has written the teen series Fear Street and the funny series Rotten School, as well as the Mostly Ghostly series, The Nightmare Room series, and the two-book thriller *Dangerous Girls*. R.L. Stine lives in New York with his wife, Jane, and Minnie, his King Charles spaniel. You can learn more about him at www.RLStine.com.

THE SCARIEST

PLACE ON EARTH!

NEED MORE THRILLS?

Get Goosebumps!

PLAY

WATCH

LISTEN

SCHOLASTIC
www.scholastic.com/goosebumps

THIS BOOK IS YOUR TICKET TO

www.EnterHorrorLand.com

CHECKLIST #10

- [ ] Inspector Cranium has a BONE to pick with your BRAIN. Can you resist?

- [ ] WARNING! You've entered the Doom Slide! Will you beat the odds?

- [ ] Watch out for the tombstones—and what's UNDER them!

- [ ] Uh-oh, the Purple Rage is VERY angry. Can you STOMP his STROGANOFF?

- [ ] Dr. Maniac has gotten everyone HEATED up. Try and cool down—but don't get TOO cool!

USER NAME

_____

PASSWORD

NOW WITH BONUS FEATURES!

For more frights, check out the Goosebumps HorrorLand video game!